An excerpt from Burn For You

She bolted upright, clutching Master's pillow to her front. The motion and noise shook Mephisto awake.

"Are you okay?" he asked, reaching for her.

She backed away from his hands and tumbled off the edge of the bed, then scrambled to her feet, still hiding behind the pillow. Last night, she'd wanted to be nude because her Master preferred her that way. Now she felt like Eve in the garden, horribly aware and suddenly ashamed of her nakedness. She didn't want to be seen, not by *him*. "Why are you here?" she asked, voice trembling.

He blinked, still coming awake. "You told me not to leave. I didn't want to leave, in case you needed me."

She meant, *Why are you here in his bed? With me?* Not that Mephisto didn't know her intimately, every inch of her. Master Mephisto and Molly had a long and complex relationship, to include a week of sex and training she'd never forget. She couldn't be around him, couldn't look at him without remembering. He had affected her that deeply, but she didn't want to remember that right now. She respected Mephisto. She knew he was her Master's closest friend, both in the scene and out.

But she wasn't ready to belong to anyone but her Master, not yet.

By

Annabel Joseph

Other erotic romance by Annabel Joseph

Mercy
Cait and the Devil
Firebird
Deep in the Woods
Fortune
Owning Wednesday
Lily Mine
Comfort Object
Caressa's Knees
Odalisque
Cirque du Minuit

Erotica by Annabel Joseph

Club Mephisto
Molly's Lips: Club Mephisto Retold

Coming soon:

Command Performance
The Edge of the Earth (as Molly Joseph)
Disciplining the Duchess

For Ingrid,
for encouraging me when I thought this was
impossible.

And for my husband...these books
are all a love song for you.

CHAPTER ONE
THIS DAY

Molly paused in the midst of her violin practice, subduing the urge to hurl the instrument across the room. *Breathe in, breathe out. Master wants this. You serve your Master. Suck it up.*

This was all Mephisto's fault. If he was here right now, she'd happily smash her violin over his head. Master hadn't been after Molly to improve herself until she'd gone to stay with Master Mephisto for a week. Then, suddenly, after a few meetings with Mephisto, her Master had decided she needed to put her mind to something challenging besides serving him.

The thing was, Molly was perfectly happy just serving him. She hadn't understood her Master's sudden desire to "broaden her horizons" as he put it. It sounded suspiciously like something Mephisto might say. Master had finally decided Molly should apply herself to learning an instrument so he could relax and listen to her play in the evenings. Molly had suggested the triangle or tambourine, but Master had rejected those ideas and bought her a violin. A thirty thousand dollar violin.

Talk about pressure.

Sure, Master liked to spoil her, but a thirty thousand dollar violin was a little over the top, especially since she'd never played an instrument in her life. The first six months had been excruciating, both for Molly and Master. She lived to please him, but in this, she fell short. Even twice weekly lessons with a violinist from the City Orchestra couldn't inject any talent into her clumsy fingers. Her failure was a constant pain, made worse by her Master's tireless encouragement. He wouldn't let her give up. When she finally realized he wouldn't let her bail out, she did slowly start to get better.

Now, two years later, she was adequate at the instrument, but not good by any means. Not good enough for Master.

Thanks, Mephisto.

Of course, when Master took her to Mephisto's elite BDSM club, the irksome man always made a point of asking how her lessons were going. It worried her that her Master and Mephisto remained such close friends, frequently lunching together. She imagined these lunches as nothing more than pow-wows in which they plotted ways to drive her insane. The violin in her hands was proof enough of that.

"Girl!" Mrs. Jernigan yelled from downstairs. "You can leave off that infernal racket. It's five o'clock."

Molly turned to the door and squelched the urge to make a nasty face. The grouchy old housekeeper couldn't see her anyway, and Master wouldn't like it. He preferred that she behave with grace and decorum. She'd learned early in their marriage that childish or petty behavior was strictly punished, usually with a cane. She would have to stand and listen to a sharp, emphatic lecture, then describe exactly what she'd done to be punished for. She always felt two inches tall as he glared through her recitation. Then, he'd deliver the brisk command to bend over. When she was sniffling and crying with ten red stripes across her ass, she'd have to stand and thank him, sincerely, for correcting her.

Well, sincerity was never a problem. She was grateful for his guiding hand, even when it hurt her so badly she couldn't sit down. It was her behavior that troubled her, like her impatience with the violin. She knew when Master got home, she'd have to admit she'd lost her temper in practice, that she'd wanted to smash the priceless instrument he'd gifted her with. How spoiled of her. She deserved to be punished for it.

At least she hadn't made the face at Mrs. Jernigan. "Girl!" came her voice again, like nails on a chalkboard. All right. Damn. Now she'd made a face. It wasn't her best day, but Master accepted all her weaknesses, corrected them, and moved on. Perhaps later, if he saw fit to punish her and she took it well, he would reward her with sex. Molly loved when her Master made love to her, even when he was rough or hurt her. Just as often, he was gentle and attentive. He loved to make her come.

Molly carried the violin to its case and carefully laid it within the velvet lining. It was valued at thirty thousand dollars, sure, but it was priceless to her, because it had been a gift from her Master, just like the slim metal eternity collar around her neck. Her collar was designed to pass for a piece of jewelry to the vanilla world, but it was so much more than that. It was the only thing she wore on a day-to-day basis, the only thing she wanted to wear. Her Master wanted her bare to his gaze, so that's how she was happiest. She couldn't remember the last time she'd worn clothes in the house. Perhaps at Clayton's annual holiday party a couple months ago. Her yearly opportunity to be snubbed and side-eyed by his vicious, holier-than-thou family.

Ugh, what was wrong with her today? Another transgression to confess—nasty thoughts about his sisters and their jerky husbands, and his stodgy old mother with her old-bat wrinkled face. Master would agree with her that his family was nasty but he'd still punish her, because it wasn't genteel to think such thoughts. Wow, she was going to get her ass beaten.

She closed the violin case and proceeded resolutely downstairs, before Mrs. Jernigan could scream "Girl!" again in her abrasive voice. The housekeeper took her arm none too gently as soon as she arrived. For a tiny woman she had a good grip.

"It's about time. Should I tell your Master you're dawdling around today?"

Why not? Molly thought silently as Mrs. Jernigan nudged her onto the scale. On top of everything else Molly had to confess to him...sure, dawdling. She lifted her arms so Mrs. Jernigan could measure her waist and hips with her tape measure. The housekeeper recorded all these numbers—to the quarter inch—in a small ledger kept in a desk by the kitchen door. Molly didn't think Master ever looked at it, but she knew if she deviated from Master's desired weight and physical dimensions, Mrs. Jernigan would be the first to let him know. Fortunately, Molly's weight and figure had remained largely unchanged over the years of their marriage. Perhaps because her Master also controlled how and when she exercised and what she ate.

Mmm, *Duck a l'orange* tonight. Her favorite. She always dined alone earlier in the evening, so she could focus all her attention on him once he arrived home. It was important. Her Master worked hard, sometimes even on the weekends, and what little time they had together she dedicated completely to pleasing him, which in turn pleased Molly. It wasn't only his authority she loved. He was handsome too, fit for a fifty year old, with a full head of blond hair that barely showed any gray. He was tall, with light blue eyes that could be hard as ice or warm as a balmy summer day.

Molly took slow bites, chewing, thinking a little sadly that she'd probably receive some icy stares tonight. To even think about smashing the violin... She would have to practice harder. She would promise Master after he punished her, when he let her make her pretty little speech about doing better, that she would practice twice as hard going forward to make it up to him. That thought comforted her. Master would understand. Above everything else, he was merciful. He accepted her as she was, which was why she loved him so much it hurt her sometimes. Literally hurt her. She'd lie in bed beside him—if she'd been permitted to sleep in his bed—or on her pallet on the floor if she wasn't, and ache with love for him.

It was like her life was split into two sections, before Master and after Master. She'd met her Master when she was in her early twenties. She was thirty now, but her years of courtship and marriage to Master were all she thought about, not her previous life. Her previous life was like some dream, or nightmare, fading a little more each year.

The duck was delicious, as always. Molly took a few bites of salad and drank the milk Master insisted on, even though she didn't like it. It was Friday and Master would be home soon. A whole weekend with him. She hoped he didn't have to work over the weekend, but if he did, she'd deal with it. She'd use the time to practice!

Mrs. Jernigan poked her head in, her glance clearly broadcasting that she thought Molly was "dawdling" again. But Master liked when Molly ate slowly and sedately. Sometimes he'd take her out to an expensive restaurant and it was like being in heaven for two or three hours. They'd linger over course after course, wine and coffee and dessert, and he would give her that look across the table, that look that expressed such mastery and ownership, but kindness and sexiness too.

Molly placed her napkin beside her plate. Mrs. Jernigan came in to clear the table and take the plates back to the cook, who would then turn around and begin preparing Master's dinner. Molly heard that Master paid the cook a lot. He probably paid Mrs. Jernigan a lot too, to keep quiet about the lifestyle they shared. "Hurry, girl," the old woman said. "Go wash and do something with that hair of yours. Then you can read in the living room until your Master's on the way up."

Master always buzzed Mrs. Jernigan when he got to the lobby of their building so Molly would know to get in position to greet him at the door. It was her absolute favorite time of day, when Mrs. Jernigan yelled "He's coming!" and Molly would put away her book and hurry over to the foyer to kneel the way he'd taught her. Legs spread, hands in her lap, head bowed submissively. A slave pose, but to her, it was her Master's pose. "Why do you wait with your legs spread, girl?" he would quiz her sometimes.

"Because my body belongs to you, Master," she'd answer. "All of it."

"And why do you bow your head?"

"Because I'm your slave."

Oh, God. Molly couldn't think about those conversations or she'd have to add the crime of touching herself to her already-too-long list of trespasses. She curled her legs under her and read the book Master had set out for her, an obscure title about the history of China. He chose a wide variety of books for her to read, so that sometimes Molly felt like her head was full of strange, disjointed knowledge. No matter. If he wanted her to read it, she read it. She concentrated on the dense, scholarly text in case he chose to test her understanding. Her fingers traced over her smooth metal collar as she turned page after page. She became so engrossed that she startled when Mrs. Jernigan appeared beside her to click on a stronger light.

Molly looked around in confusion. "What time is it?"

"Nearly seven. Your Master's late, but it's Friday. Maybe he's having dinner or drinks with a friend."

"Maybe," Molly said. She wished he was here though. She felt unsettled and irritable. Something about this day just didn't feel right.

* * * * *

Mephisto received the call at five in the afternoon. He'd always remember the time, and the voice of the hospital official, frank but sympathetic. Clayton Copeland kept a card in his wallet naming Mephisto as his emergency contact. Mephisto knew he might get this call one day, but he'd hoped it would be a lot later. Decades later. Clay was only fifty years old.

Mephisto raced across town, but he was too late. The doctor spoke with him briefly, explaining a lot of medical stuff while Mephisto stared at the still form on the hospital bed. Clayton didn't look like himself. It was strange, how quickly the life force fled once the body was gone. It should have lingered a while, especially in someone as powerful and vibrant as him. It should have seeped away slowly, so it wasn't such a shock to see him lying there. So Mephisto could have had the time to say goodbye. It wasn't right for a great man like Clayton Copeland to die alone.

The sterile medical words roiled around in Mephisto's brain as he sat at Clay's bedside trying to make sense of things. Ruptured cerebral aneurysm. Stroke, seizure, death. The doctor spoke to Mephisto as if he might have expected this. The bulging vessel in Clay's brain had been diagnosed almost two years earlier, at a medical center in New York. They'd had difficulty placing a stent. Didn't Mephisto know about any of this?

No. All Mephisto knew was that almost two years earlier, Clay had called and asked him to look after Molly for a week so he could take a "business trip." Mephisto remembered Clay making a flurry of abrupt legal preparations around that time. He remembered a strange conversation at a park afterward, a secretive expression clouding the man's face.

If I die tomorrow, tell her you love her.

I would give her to you now if I wasn't so selfish.

Why had Clayton kept this secret from them? Because he was a very unselfish man. He hadn't wanted them to carry the burden of worry about a condition that couldn't be fixed. Mephisto could have handled it, but Molly would have been beside herself with fear and anxiety.

Molly.

Mephisto looked at his watch and then buried his hands in his dreadlocks. It was nearly seven. Molly would be wondering where Clay was, why her Master wasn't home yet. What now? He'd promised Clayton he'd take care of Molly in the event of his death, and he would, but Mephisto had never really thought past the general idea of the thing, and he certainly hadn't expected it to happen so soon. Hell, of course he'd take care of her, but he'd never thought about the specifics, like how on earth he was supposed to look Molly in the eyes and tell her that her Master was gone. Then there were all the other things he'd have to help her with...funeral arrangements, dealing with Clayton's family and his multi-million dollar estate. Clayton had multiple businesses and foundations, and real estate from coast to coast, all of it Molly's now.

Later. Mephisto would think about all that later or he'd get overwhelmed. For now, he had to go to Molly, and he had to figure out what to say when he got there, because they weren't the kind of words you could come up with on the fly. *Molly...your Master died today.* That part was easy, but what would he say then? He'd have to bring her to the hospital. She would need to say goodbye, even though it would be heart wrenching for her to see Clayton lying there lifeless. Mephisto was all too familiar with the still, unsettling face of death, but it struck deeper when it was a friend. For Molly...

Oh, God.

Mephisto stood and straightened his shoulders. He could finish his breakdown later. For now, he had to be strong enough for both of them. He drove to Clayton's high rise, sitting in traffic beside other cars containing people going through the everyday grind. Going home perhaps, after a day of work. Looking forward to dinner or a night on the town. Fuck, it was Friday. He called Josh at the club, asked him to manage events for the night. It seemed bizarre that while he was driving over to wreck Molly's world, everyone else was going about their usual business and the employees of his fetish club were showing up for a typical night of work.

Mephisto took the elevator up to Clay's floor, took the long walk down the hall. He'd only been to Clay's gleaming castle in the sky a few times. He stopped outside the formidable front door, rubbed his temple and took a deep breath. His knock brought the housekeeper. Mephisto couldn't remember her name. She took one look at his face, though, and she knew.

"I need to see Molly," he said.

The housekeeper stepped back and let him in. Molly was perched on a chair in the living room. He could see her from the foyer, her dark head bent over a book.

"Mr. Copeland died today," he said to the old woman. "A couple hours ago."

He'd spoken quietly but Molly looked up at the sound of his voice. For a moment, the most fleeting moment, she looked happy to see him, like anyone might look when they saw a friend. But then, perhaps from the look on his face, she understood something was wrong. She came to him and her sudden distress, her nakedness, none of it registered with him. Just that gleaming collar around her neck.

"Molly, it's Clayton. Your Master. Your husband."

He reached out to her, took her hand. Her voice trembled when she asked, "What? What is it?"

He couldn't say anything more for a moment with the tension in his throat. He swallowed hard and squeezed her fingers. "I'm so sorry. He had a stroke. They took him to the hospital. He started having seizures."

Tears filled Molly's blue eyes. "Oh, no. Poor Master."

He kept staring at her, too weak to say the next words. Her gaze begged for more information, but at the same time, she looked afraid to ask. "Well?" she finally managed. "Did they fix him? He's okay, isn't he?"

Mephisto shook his head. "He's not okay. He died around five o'clock this evening. I'm so sorry." They were such inadequate words. He embraced her, meaning to comfort her, but she went wooden, rigid. She pulled back and shook her head.

"That can't be. He was perfectly fine this morning. There's got to be some mistake."

"No, Molly."

"Another patient. Mistaken identity."

"It's not a mistake," he said. "I've just come from there. If you want to go see him, I'll take you. You should probably go see him one last time."

Still she stared at him. She didn't believe. He turned back to Mrs. Jernigan, standing near the foyer wringing her hands. The frail woman shook her head at Mephisto and ran away, into some back hallway. Molly stood like a statue, her hands pressed to her mouth.

"I can't believe it. No," she said.

"I'm sorry."

"No."

"I'm here to help you. I promised Clayton I'd help you if anything ever happened to him."

He reached out to touch her but she skirted his grasp, turning her back on him. He watched her draw in deep breaths, her slender shoulders rising and falling. She shook her head, a small, hypnotic movement.

Denial. First step.

"Honey." He moved closer to her again. "Do you have clothes to put on? I'm afraid if you don't see him one last time to say goodbye, you'll regret it later. It's up to you, but—" His voice cut off. He was giving her choices, which was probably the last thing she could handle at the moment, this girl whose choices were all made for her by the man who'd died.

"Where are your clothes?" Mephisto asked instead. "Please get dressed."

"He has them," she said. "My Master."

"In his room?" Mephisto set off down the hallway. Molly came after him, grabbing his arm.

"He doesn't let me in there. Not without him."

He stopped and turned to her. "Listen, Molly. Your Master left you in my care. I'm taking you to the hospital to say goodbye and sign papers and do all the things a wife has to do. You owe him this, to do things the right way." His voice was sharper than he'd intended. She paled and stepped back while he continued down the hall. A moment later, he heard her behind him. He barged into Clay's bedroom and paused. Pristine, as he'd expected it to be.

Molly stepped aside as the housekeeper pushed through, the wrinkles beneath her eyes damp with silent tears. "I'll get some things together for Mr. Copeland. He would want his best clothes. His favorite cufflinks and shoes."

"Thank you," Mephisto said.

Molly stood at the door, eyes wide, while the housekeeper moved around the room gathering items for Clayton.

"I'm sorry," Mephisto said. "I don't remember your name."

"Rose Jernigan. I've been his housekeeper for twenty years. It's not right, him gone so soon. He'll be missed." She clamped her lips shut then, running a lint brush over a black wool suit.

16

"Mrs. Jernigan, I need to know where he kept Molly's clothes."

"She's got plenty of clothes in the second closet. Very nice things." She pointed to a door adjacent to the bathroom. Mephisto found another full dressing room.

He turned to Molly. "Come pick something out. What did he like you to wear? Did he have a favorite outfit?"

Mephisto just wanted to give her something to think about besides the tears choking her, and Mrs. Jernigan's somber work collecting Clayton's clothes. Molly crossed to a bureau and took out panties and a bra, and smooth stockings with lace at the top. He could see her fingers shaking from across the room. Mephisto turned away and let her dress, helping Mrs. Jernigan pack Clayton's things in a high-end travel bag. "Will you come?" he asked the housekeeper. "You're welcome to come with us."

She hesitated and shook her head. "I'll need to get the house in order for callers. Have you told his family?"

"If you have their contact information, you should call them. They can call his lawyers and business partners. Everyone will need to know."

A stifled sob sounded from the closet. They both turned. The more Molly dressed, the harder she cried, and the bleaker Mephisto felt. She pulled a dark cardigan over a silk shell and fumbled with the placket. Mephisto crossed to her and fastened the row of small black buttons one by one. Then Molly went to an ornate wooden jewelry box and opened the lid. So many priceless pieces for a wife who probably only wore clothes a handful of times a year. Mephisto helped her put on a pearl necklace and earrings, thinking of Clayton and his love for her. It was so unfair. *So* unfair. Couples that loved so hard should have forever together.

"I can't...I can't do this," she whispered. "I can't do this. I can't do this."

"You don't have a choice," Mephisto said, kindly but firmly. "I'm sorry, but you don't."

CHAPTER TWO
CHOICES

At the hospital, Molly touched Clayton's cold, still hand and drew away. It was only then, Mephisto thought, that she finally believed. She stared and cried, and stared and cried, refusing to leave but unable to get more than a foot or two closer. "I want him back," she said to Mephisto at one point. "I want him back. I don't want this!"

Anger. Second step.

And there was still a lot of disbelief. Molly stared as if she expected Clay to somehow revive himself. He was her all-powerful, unflappable Master, after all. Finally, Mephisto had to make her leave so the funeral home could come. One last time, Molly touched Clay's hand. Still cold. Still dead. His heart ached for her.

He took her back to the home she and Clayton had shared, and his heart ached harder. Molly's whole life had revolved around serving Clay, and now that he wasn't there, she floated like a ghost lost in the wrong plane. She wouldn't let Mephisto come near, wouldn't let Mrs. Jernigan comfort her either, although the old woman puttered around with tea and refreshments, none of which were touched. Molly finally settled on the edge of the couch, pulling at her clothes, looking at the door. Waiting.

"Molly, I know this is terrible for you," Mephisto finally said, "but he's not coming back."

"I know that. I'm not stupid."

He and Mrs. Jernigan exchanged glances. He replied to her snapped retort with utter calm. "It's late. I know it won't be easy to sleep, but you should try."

"But my Master's not here," she said, as if Mephisto were an idiot.

Molly needed sleep. She was stretched to the breaking point. Her mind was rebelling against a reality she didn't want to accept, even as tears flowed down her cheeks.

Mephisto stood. "Come on." He held out his hand but she wouldn't take it. She finally rose from the couch and went before him. She washed her face, brushed her teeth, took off her clothes as if in a trance, hung up the garments neatly. She took off her jewelry, placed it away with care. Then she moved toward the bed and froze.

"What's wrong?"

"I can't. It's his bed. He didn't say I could."

Mephisto sighed. "Molly—"

"You don't understand. Every night, he told me, sleep here. Or sleep there." She pointed to a pallet on the floor.

"He's not here tonight. He can't tell you those things anymore. Just get in his bed, lie down and rest. That's what he would have told you to do."

She climbed in, quickly, guiltily, like she was breaking some rule. She promptly burst into tears again. "It smells like him."

For half an hour more, Mephisto held her as she sobbed. She was conflicted, turning toward and away from him in dizzying changes of mood. She spilled out watersheds of words. *It's not fair. I don't understand. What am I going to do? Who will plan the funeral? Where is his body right now?* By the time he quieted her, Mephisto was exhausted himself. He pulled the covers up over her.

"Where are you going?" She grasped at him as he stood.

"Nowhere. Just back out to the living room."

"Don't go. Don't leave. I'm sorry."

He sat back down. "Sorry for what?"

"You're mad at me, I know. I'm sorry, I'm just—"

"Hey, hey." He stroked her arm, only to have her pull away from him—and then look guilty for pulling away. "I'm not mad, not even one percent mad," he assured her. "I'm one hundred percent worried and sad for you, though, and I want you to sleep and let your mind rest. You're going to need a lot of strength to get through the next few days."

"Don't leave," she cried again.

So he stayed until she fell asleep, thinking back to Clayton's words during their conversation a couple years ago. *See, that's the thing. I don't think she'll be fine. Not emotionally, or any way else.*

Jay, if I die, I want you to take care of her. I mean, watch out for her. You know what I mean.

This is what Clayton had meant. As part of their consensual TPE relationship, Clay had taken away so much of her freedom, so much of her autonomy, that he'd known she wouldn't be able to function when he was gone. This is what that looked like, this conflict and terror. Mephisto understood now why Clayton had been so worried. What a fucking mess.

Once she was asleep, her face relaxed from the tension of grieving, Mephisto returned to the living room to drink Irish whiskey with Mrs. Jernigan and figure out what to do next.

Mrs. Jernigan—Rose, as he called her now that they were drinking together—seemed to have shed most of her tears. She was all business, thinking over the most important matters, like who she would have to contact in the morning, and what she needed to do to prepare the house for family and guests. She took the phone calls as they came, making copious notes on who was arriving when, so Clayton's driver could pick them up.

"You'll have to handle Molly," Mephisto warned her. "Once the family starts to descend, I won't be able to hang around and manage her through this transition. Not without causing a lot of questions about Clayton's private life."

Rose looked skeptical. "I'm not sure I can handle that one."

"It's just until after the funeral. Until his family leaves town. From what I understand they were never that close. I doubt they'll stay long."

"They'll stay long enough to make Mrs. Copeland uncomfortable. They'll want her to take herself off, now Mr. Copeland's gone."

"They can't make her leave. This is her house now." He topped off the housekeeper's glass and then leaned back in his chair with a sigh. "Will you stay on here? You won't leave her, will you? She's going to need you, and not just as a housekeeper."

Mrs. Jernigan looked apologetic, but resolute. "I'm afraid I can't stay. Not beyond the funeral. I'll stay until Mr. Copeland's laid to rest, until his family leaves, but then I'll be off. I don't know that she'd want me to stay anyway. I'd have left years ago if not for the generous salary. I never much liked how he treated that woman. Like an animal, making her go around naked and collared, and she putting up with it, so pleased with herself. I didn't agree at all with how they got on together. I don't care to stay around and see her with another just the same." She slid him a look. "Will you be the next one, then?"

Mephisto went still. Would he be the next one? Subconsciously, he supposed he'd been mulling over that question. He wanted Molly as much as he ever had, and Clayton had assumed Molly would go to him next. Hell, he'd practically pushed her into Mephisto's arms. There'd been an understanding between them, but like everything else, the details were a lot more complicated than the general idea.

"I don't know," he said to Rose, pouring more whiskey into his own glass. "I don't know if I'll be the next one or not. I guess that will be up to Molly."

"Agh, like she can make a decision, that one. If you don't snap her up, someone else will, and she'll go following after him like she doesn't have a brain between her ears."

"She has a brain," Mephisto said a little sharply.

Rose nodded and waved a hand. "I know. Don't get your dander up. Believe me, I know. That's the most irritating thing about it. No, I won't stay. Not past a week or so, to get things settled. I owe Mr. Copeland that at least. Then I'll retire, thanking him for so many years of generosity."

She sighed and got to her feet. "I'm for bed. Will you stay tonight? There's a guest bedroom down the hall from Mr. Copeland's room."

"Yes, I'll stay." Mephisto wouldn't dream of leaving Molly alone tonight. He wouldn't stay in the guest room either. *Will you be the next one, then?* He couldn't think about that yet. Like everything else, it was too overwhelming at the moment. Still, as confused and sad as he was, he couldn't imagine what Molly was feeling in her grief.

* * * * *

Molly woke up reaching for Master before she remembered he was gone. Her eyes ached, her throat ached. Her whole body ached with the absence of him.

And Master Mephisto was lying beside her in Master's bed.

She bolted upright, clutching Master's pillow to her front. The motion and noise shook Mephisto awake.

"Are you okay?" he asked, reaching for her.

She backed away from his hands and tumbled off the edge of the bed, then scrambled to her feet, still hiding behind the pillow. Last night, she'd wanted to be nude because her Master preferred her that way. Now she felt like Eve in the garden, horribly aware and suddenly ashamed of her nakedness. She didn't want to be seen, not by *him*. "Why are you here?" she asked, voice trembling.

He blinked, still coming awake. "You told me not to leave. I didn't want to leave, in case you needed me."

She meant, *Why are you here in his bed? With me?* Not that Mephisto didn't know her intimately, every inch of her. Master Mephisto and Molly had a long and complex relationship, to include a week of sex and training she'd never forget. She couldn't be around him, couldn't look at him without remembering. He had affected her that deeply, but she didn't want to remember that right now. She respected Mephisto. She knew he was her Master's closest friend, both in the scene and out. But she wasn't ready to belong to anyone but her Master, not yet.

But your Master's gone.

22

"It's okay, Molly," he said. "I know what you're thinking."

With anyone else, she might have doubted, but Mephisto could read her better than anyone she'd ever known in her life. Yes, including her Master. She burst into tears. "I'm sorry. I don't... I want... I know you're just trying to help but I don't want—"

He held out a hand, but he didn't come closer. Maybe he thought she'd attack with Master's pillow. She buried her face in it instead.

"I'm just here to help," he said. "That's all. I promised your Master I'd look after you. That means whatever you want it to mean." His kind, calm voice somehow made things seem even bleaker.

"I don't know what anything means right now," she bawled. "I don't know what I'm going to do."

"You're going to grieve for a while." Mephisto got out of bed, approached her slowly. "Can I hold you? I'd really like to comfort you right now, as a friend. Your Master would want me to comfort you."

"My Master's not here!" she screamed. As quickly as it flared, her explosion of rage died, and she clawed at the pillow in misery. "I'm sorry. I'm sorry..."

"Shhh." Mephisto put an arm around her, then another, and she was crying into his chest, soaking his dark tee shirt. "I'm just here as a friend," he said. "For as long as you need me. You're going to need a friend."

She backed away from him. "It's hard to think of you as a friend, Master Mephisto."

"Don't 'Master' me then. Just call me Mephisto for a while. How can I help you? Right now, what can I do? Do you want to get dressed, have some breakfast? Clayton's family will show up soon. I don't want to be here, but I can help you get ready. Mrs. Jernigan can help if you'd rather."

Still Molly stood, her Master's pillow dangling from her hand. She hugged it to herself again. She didn't know what to do, how to go on beyond standing there. Yes, she had to get dressed. Yes, she ought to eat, although the idea of it nauseated her. She would have to keep living, but it seemed an insurmountable task even to make her legs move.

"Why won't you be here?" she asked Mephisto. "You said you'd help me. They'll try to make me leave. They'll try to cut me out, separate me from Master."

"They won't." He shook his head brusquely. "Don't let them. Clay left everything to you. It's all in his will, ironclad. They have no right to anything, no right to even come in this house unless you let them. Remember that." He moved closer. His dark eyes shone with kindness. Understanding. "I know you've been a slave for years now. You can be a slave again if you want to, in time. But for now, for this time right now, you need to be strong. You need to stand up for yourself and Clayton, and plan his funeral and settle his affairs. I know it sounds impossible, that you think you won't be able to do it, but you'll have help."

"You said you wouldn't be here."

"Just for now, while his family's around. I think I might scare them," he said with a slight smile. Molly thought it was probably true. The large, muscular, pierced and tattooed black man would probably stand out a bit too much amidst Clayton's lily white relatives. "Besides, no one can know about Clayton's fetish life. You and I know, of course. The Seattle fetish community knows, but they'll be discreet. His household staff knows but they'll be discreet too. His family..." He pinned her with a direct gaze. "His family can't know, so you can't be the slave right now. You have to be the wife. Mrs. Molly Copeland. You'll have help from his executors and lawyers. Lots of people will give you advice. Listen to them."

Molly felt sick terror in her stomach. "How will I know I can trust them?"

"If Clayton trusted them, it's a safe bet you can trust them."

Of course. Her Master had been an excellent judge of character. He would have surrounded himself with the most trustworthy business partners. And her Master had told her outright, many times, that he didn't trust his family, so Molly wouldn't trust them either. Her Master trusted Mephisto...so she would have to trust him.

"I think I'll get dressed," she said. "I'm sure you have to go. The club..."

"Club Mephisto will be fine. But if you feel okay at the moment, I'll go and take care of a few things." He came to her and squeezed her hand. Molly couldn't look at his face, so she didn't know what his expression was. Sad, probably. Pitying. As soon as he was gone, she allowed herself to fall apart yet again, collapsing where she stood, sobbing until her eyes and head ached so much she had to stop. *This is too hard. This is too hard, Master. Please, come back. I'll be good, so good if you do.*

But no matter how good she was, or how perfect, this was all she had left at the end of it. Nothing.

Nothing at all.

* * * * *

Mephisto sat in the back of the sprawling city church at Clayton's funeral, feeling uncomfortable in his suit and tie. He'd said his goodbyes to Clayton beside the hospital bed, but he wouldn't have missed this. Clayton would have been happy with the grand, polished service, even though he was never a religious man. Clayton had always been very much about appearances and decorum, even though he accepted Mephisto's scruffy goth image. *Clayton, man, you should see me in this suit.*

Mephisto didn't know how Molly was coping. He hadn't done any more than talk on the phone with Mrs. Jernigan the last few days. Molly didn't have a phone. No email address, no nothing. He could barely see the back of her bowed head where she sat in the front row.

Later, at the graveside service, Mephisto was able to study her more closely. Beneath her smart black suit, her widow's hat, she looked like a shell of the Molly he knew. An imposter. Clayton's family, at least, seemed to be tending to her. She stood between two of his sisters, looking for all the world as wealthy and brittle as they were. He understood that Molly was in a tunnel now, in the dark. She had gone into the tunnel from Clayton's light, and would come out of it some day, blinking and confused. For now, the tunnel probably felt like a safe place.

Molly raised her head, looked up at him. Their eyes locked. She must have felt him staring.

If I die tomorrow, tell her you love her.

Clayton had known he might die. For two years, he had kept that secret. As for the other secret...that Mephisto loved his wife... Clay had sensed that too, and been okay with it. But Molly...she hadn't known anything.

There was no way she could know. Mephisto wasn't sure of his feelings himself. He always insisted to Clay it was only because of their long history that he took such an interest in her. Mephisto had known Molly in her pre-slave years, when she'd been a wild, tormented young woman. He flattered himself into believing he'd saved her from that. Mephisto liked feeling powerful, liked the idea that he'd somehow had a hand in making her a new person. But the truth was, he had very little to do with creating the complex person who was Molly.

As quickly as their eyes met, Molly looked away. Mephisto couldn't read her face. He only knew there was grief there, and emptiness. *What do I do, Clay?*

Mephisto could go for it. Wait a few weeks, until the worst of her grief had passed, and lay it all on the line, tell Molly his true feelings. *I would like to be your next Master. I want you under my hand. I want that incredible submission you gave to Clayton, all for myself now.* He did desperately want her to serve him. He loved her beauty, her calmness. Her deep feelings of worship and fidelity to her Master. But could he earn those feelings? She couldn't just summon them up from nothing. Clayton Copeland had earned every iota of Molly's admiration and love. Mephisto understood it wouldn't be easy to fill Clay's shoes.

Then there was his own life to think about. He had Club Mephisto to run, and a lot of s-types who counted on him as an occasional play partner. What did it look like, if Molly came into his life? She could be his alpha-slave, sure, ranking above the others, but would that be enough for her? Could Mephisto participate in playful scene-type slavery relationships with his other partners and still demand the depth of Molly's service? Molly's...love? Mephisto had never been in a romantic-love relationship that wasn't connected to power exchange or sex. What made him think he could fulfill Molly, with a history like that?

It all came down to worthiness, something he'd never questioned in himself. Well, no, he'd questioned it before, during the one week Molly had stayed with him two years ago. That week had forced him to face many truths about himself, not all of them pleasant.

That was the week he'd fallen for her like a boulder off a cliff.

But boulders could smash people. He'd tried very hard, in a way, to smash her that week, and she remembered. Of course she remembered. Her Master's wishes aside, it was very possible she dreaded nothing more than ending up in Mephisto's hands.

After the graveside service, everyone drifted away from the yawning hole in the ground, but Molly lingered, and so did Mephisto. For a while he kept his distance, watching her, trying to gauge if he was welcome. She stared down into the earth, thinking about God knew what. The man she loved, probably, cold now in the ground.

"Molly." Mephisto approached her, feeling very much like a supplicant. Her eyes traveled over him, over his suit and wool overcoat.

"Hello. Thanks for coming today." She bit her lip. "Thank you for the flowers. Tulips were his favorite."

"I know." She was trying too hard to sound cheerful. It unsettled him. "How are you?"

"Oh...." She shrugged, still in that fake-cheerful tone. "I've been better. I was actually going to call you after the funeral. I've been thinking."

Mephisto stepped closer, feeling nervousness snake up his spine at her unfamiliar briskness, her closed expression. "Thinking about what?"

She let out a long, shuddery sigh. "About my life."

"Molly!" One of Clayton's sisters called out to her. "Are you okay? Shall we hold the car?"

Mephisto looked at the woman, then back at Molly. "I'll drive you back if you like. If you want to stay and talk."

"Well... Okay."

"I mean, if you've been thinking about your life, this might be a long conversation."

Molly turned to Clayton's sister and waved. "I'm going to stay a little while longer."

The woman looked between him and Molly. Sure, his clothes were spiffy, but he still had dreadlocks and a stud in his nose. He smiled and walked over. "I'm Jay Tennant. An old friend of Clayton's."

"Oh?" Her *oh?* was clearly a request for more information.

Mephisto gave a short glance at Molly. "I used to do security for one of Clay's properties." The woman wouldn't understand the real meaning of that, but it was more or less the truth. Security work would also explain his build and appearance. She offered him a lackluster handshake.

"I'm Margaret Kearney. One of Clayton's sisters."

"I see the resemblance," Mephisto said.

Margaret Kearney looked like she had plenty more questions, but she didn't ask them. Instead she turned to Molly, wearing a tight smile. "Don't be too long. We'll be receiving visitors back at the house."

Molly didn't answer, only stared down into Clayton's grave. With one last look at Mephisto, the woman turned and stalked across the grass to a waiting car. Mephisto swallowed down unkind cracks about Mrs. Kearney, in deference to Molly's pensive mood. "We can stay here as long as you like," he said. "As long as it takes to say goodbye."

"To you?" She looked confused.

"No. To Clayton. To your Master."

"I've already said goodbye." She frowned and gave another little shrug. "He's not there anyway. I know that. All of this is just for show."

Mephisto waited. He knew there was more. Molly brushed aside the black tulle shielding her face and held her forehead like she had an ache there.

"Okay, listen," she said. "I know you and my...Mr. Copeland had an agreement. That, you know, after he died I would go to you."

Mephisto shook his head. "That wasn't the agreement. I only promised to look after you. What you do with your life now is up to you, fully and completely."

"So...that's what I've been thinking about."

"Good."

"And I see now what you were trying to show me that week we spent together. That day in the kitchen, that last day when you asked me all those questions. I get it now. I understand how stupid I've been, how all of this has been so bad and wrong."

Mephisto stiffened. Those words were the last words he'd expected to fall from Molly's lips. "I don't know what you're talking about. That day when I asked you those questions, I was only trying to make sure you were happy."

"Bullshit." She pursed her lips, her pretty face distorting in anger. "You took me out to that park where I used to work. You fed me ice cream and led me to that creek and you stared at me. I remember. You did everything you could to...to break me down. I see now you were trying to snap me out of it."

"I wasn't. You are absolutely, one hundred percent wrong."

"But I was so blind," she said over his protestations. "I was so deep under his spell."

"Molly, you have everything so wrong."

"Do I?" She turned from him, staring off into the distance, her chin set. "It's taken a few days, and a few tears, but my brain finally started working again. I'm ashamed. I'm disgusted by the lifestyle I led. Eight years his slave, for what?"

"Because it made you happy." She was silent a moment. Mephisto was glad she wasn't denying that, at least. "He made you happy, and you made him happy. Don't rewrite your time together as something disgusting and sordid. That's very disrespectful to him, to his memory."

"I don't owe him respect anymore," she snapped, moving away from the graveside. "I don't owe him service, or sex, or obedience or any of that stupid shit. He's dead, and I'm left with nothing but eight years of my life lost."

Through his shock, through his anger at her words, he remembered that grief could mess with people. She didn't mean any of this. She couldn't mean it. "Nothing? He left you with *nothing*? He left you everything."

"Money, houses." She waved a hand. "Whatever. I want those years back. All the things he left me, were they worth what I gave him? The loss of myself? He seduced me. He used me. He erased me!"

"He loved you!" Mephisto's words rang out in the quiet cemetery. He felt the strangest impulse to weep on behalf of his friend, who had loved Molly to the point of distraction. "Who have you been talking to? Who planted these ideas in your brain?"

"No one. I've just rejoined reality."

"You're still wearing his collar."

"Because I can't get it off. I need you to help me get it off."

"No. I won't help you." He sounded as bitter as he felt. "If it means so little to you now, call a locksmith. Use a pair of fucking bolt cutters."

Molly stared at the ground, her spine rigid. "I think I'd like to go back now. Or...you can call me a cab if you'd rather."

"I'm not calling you a cab," he muttered. They walked to his car and drove together in silence for some time. He couldn't understand this. Sadness, yes. Grief and regrets, sure. But to go from deep love for Clayton to this revulsion? No. Shame? Disgust?

"I think you're all mixed up right now," Mephisto finally said. Molly shifted and sighed. "No, really. Your husband just died. Your world has been disrupted."

"Yes, it has been disrupted. Thank God. I know this upsets you. I know your whole world is tied up in all this Master and slave shit—"

"Do not call it shit." His anger resonated between them in the small car, and she fell silent beside him. Mephisto took deep breaths, in and out. "If you're done with the lifestyle, that's fine, but why don't you keep your judgments and condemnations to yourself?"

"Because you advance this. Every day, in your club, you push submissive women toward dominants. You pushed me toward Clayton.

You glamorize it like it's some divine calling, something honorable and important."

"It is! For those in the lifestyle, it is."

"It's sick. It's exploitative. Of course you and the other dominants want to color it in pretty colors, make sure your victims remain blind and subservient. How else can you abuse and sexually exploit women without them fighting back?"

Mephisto slammed on the brakes and guided the car to the side of the roadway. Traffic buzzed past, mixing with the drumbeat of fury in his brain.

"How dare you?" he asked. "How dare you accuse me of abuse? No one in this community has spoken out more about consent, about safety, about emotionally healthy relationships. Not to mention, I saved your life, you ungrateful little bitch. Do you remember where you were when I met you?"

"At some bar on Pike Street. I remember. Whatever."

"No," he said, leaning closer. "Do you remember where you were mentally, in your life, when I met you? Let me remind you. You hated your life, you hated yourself, you hated Daddy, you hated every boy you beckoned between your well-traveled thighs. You were trying to destroy yourself with alcohol and drugs and hate, and came very close to succeeding. Do you remember that?"

She sat frozen beside him, her lips set in a stubborn line. Mephisto cursed under his breath and moved back onto the road.

"You don't have to thank me," he said after a moment. "You can be angry at me for trying to help you. But let's be real. The life you gave up was no better than the life you had with Clayton."

"At least it was my life!" she retorted. "At least I was myself!"

"Don't you get it? You were yourself with Clayton too! You were at peace, you were happy. That week we spent together..." His voice faltered. "I spent the whole week testing you, questioning you, trying to be sure, and I was sure. When your Master returned for you, and he held you, and you cried, I was more sure of your love for each other than anything I'd ever been sure of in my life."

31

Mephisto fell silent. There was nothing else to say, only the truth, and he'd said it. After a long while Molly said, "I don't think you mean to abuse anyone. Not intentionally. But I think you do."

Jesus fucking Christ. "I think I don't."

"I don't think you understand how this feels, to surface after you've been held underwater for so long."

"You were never held underwater. Don't lie. You floated there yourself, with a big fucking smile on your face."

"Because I was influenced, brainwashed."

"Brainwashed. I knew that word would come." He pulled up outside Clayton's building and put the car in park, then rubbed his eyes and looked over at her.

"You know what I think? I think your view of reality is way, way out of wack right now. I understand your life has been turned upside down. I applaud your decision to reassess your goals in life and really think before you move forward. But it's unfair to my friend to paint him as a villain, an abuser. After all he gave to you, how much he loved you. How much you loved him."

She wouldn't look at him. She stared out the window. "Of course you'd only see his side. You're just like him."

Mephisto gave a mirthless, resigned laugh. "Yes, of course. Partners in crime. Brainwashing buddies. If this is your view now of him, of me, of the lifestyle, then by all means, take off your fucking collar and join the vanilla world. I wish you the best."

With those words, Molly opened the car door and left without a backward glance. So be it. Whatever made her happy. That's what Clayton had wanted for her...to make her own choices about her future. But he and Clayton had both been so, so wrong about the choices she would make.

CHAPTER THREE
SHAME

Mephisto threw himself back into his work. The Seattle fetish scene was growing, changing, and Mephisto was always working hard to be sure it was changing for the better. People in the community looked to him as a leader, and he took that responsibility seriously. He didn't just host sex parties and club nights, but also organized classes on safety and responsible techniques. BDSM and power exchange involved a lot of pleasure, but the possibility of danger too. Nothing upset him more than someone getting hurt on his watch.

Like Molly.

Mephisto brooded for weeks about the parting talk they'd had. He finally had to admit to himself that perhaps he hadn't saved her after all. That, perhaps, he'd pushed a damaged and emotionally fragile woman toward a man too powerful and charismatic for her to resist. What could he have done differently? *You could have kept her for yourself. You could have shown her a less controlling form of slavery.* But would that have been enough for her at that time in her life?

She had seemed so happy. He truly believed she'd been happy while it was going on. So, whatever guilt he felt, he had to temper it with the fact that he'd acted on what he believed was the truth. Now, truth was getting all tangled up in his brain, which was sort of crippling but sort of helpful. He could definitely use all of this upheaval to improve himself and his actions at the club and in the scene.

Mephisto also considered whether he owed it to Clayton to continue to supervise her. He decided he didn't, that Molly would only resent his presence in her life. She knew where to find him if she needed him, but if she was truly done with the lifestyle—truly *disgusted* by it as she'd said—they didn't have much more to talk about. He missed her, but the Molly he'd adored was gone anyway, replaced by a woman who saw him as an exploiter, if not an outright abuser. That part really hurt.

But Mephisto wasn't one to live in the past. It was Saturday night, his favorite night, and he was determined to funnel renewed positivity to his kinky friends. The club was practically breathing, the walls contained so much energy and lust. Club Mephisto wasn't just about getting your rocks off and going through the motions. The people who played here believed in connection and self-expression, and they cared for one another. That carefully-tended community attitude was the accomplishment of which he was most proud.

He circulated, monitoring a heavy impact scene for a while before he moved on to an equally intense, but much quieter rigging scene. The rigger wrapped rope around his nude submissive so lovingly, so carefully, outlining her breasts and making wicked little cinches for her nipples. Once she was tied, he started working over her chest with a crop. The woman moaned and pulled away on occasion, but she always presented her breasts for more. Mephisto studied her face, searching for something, anything, any clue that she wanted to be anywhere else than where she was...

"Master Mephisto?"

Mephisto turned at the sharp voice of his dungeon assistant, Glenn. "What is it?"

"A woman by the door. I think she's altered."

"If she's altered, she can't come in. You know the rules."

"I think it's Molly."

Mephisto spun toward the door. Glenn was right. It was Molly, but she barely looked like herself. Dirty, disheveled, her face and eyes swollen, probably from substance abuse. She yanked at her collar, screaming something he couldn't hear from across the room. Her eyes found his and she came storming his way, shrugging off the doorman trying to restrain her. She barreled right through a whip scene, evading injury by dumb luck.

"What the fuck is wrong with you?" Mephisto grabbed her arm and steered her to the side of the play space. "That singletail could have taken your eye out."

"Get it off me," she screamed, yanking at her neck, at the slim collar still gleaming there. "Take it off me, goddamn it. I know you know how."

The dungeon monitors were drifting closer in case Mephisto needed help, and patrons were starting to watch. Molly pulled at her collar like a full-blown maniac. She was on something, rabid, out of her mind. He dragged her back past the bar into his private rooms. He flipped on the light in the kitchen and looked down at the girl in his grasp. Her eyes were dilated, her skin pallid. She'd lost fifteen pounds at least since he saw her last. Six weeks ago?

"What are you on?" It came out a growl. Mephisto didn't allow drugs in his club and he didn't allow them in his life. "What the fuck have you been doing to yourself?"

She ignored him, pulling so hard on the collar he worried she'd injure her neck. She let out an ear rending scream. "Take it off! Get it off me!"

"Okay, I'll take it off. When you calm down, I'll take it off. Let go of it."

He took her hands, restraining her with some effort. There were garish bruises around her neck. Who knew how long she'd been trying to get it off? But pulling it right through her neck wasn't the way to do it. Her small hands struggled in his.

"Let go of me," she moaned. "Let go!"

"I'll let go when you stop fighting me. Don't touch it. I need a special tool to get it off but I won't go get it until you calm down."

She sucked in air. Some shred of awareness flickered in her eyes. Her gaze darted around his kitchen and she licked dry lips. He'd lay odds she was on some hallucinogen, not unknown for the old Molly. "Sit down," he said slowly and clearly. "Sit down and I'll take your collar off."

He led her to a chair at the table and she sank down. She shook all over, so hard he could almost hear it. She was in her usual pre-Clayton gear. Short skirt, nearly non-existent top. It was thirty degrees outside. He got a blanket from the bedroom and draped it around her. She reached again for the metal band around her neck, arrested by his disapproving sound. Glenn peeked in the door.

"Everything okay?"

"She'll be fine. Watch her a minute."

Mephisto hurried to the club's storage room, rooted through hardware and drawers of tools until he found the micro-screwdriver he needed. Molly wouldn't be the first slave he'd sprung from a "permanent" collar, nor would she be the last. He returned to the kitchen to find Molly glaring at Glenn with a murderous look.

"She's not quite herself, is she?" Glenn asked. "You want me to call anyone?"

"The loony bin?" Mephisto suggested. "Not for her. For me. No. She'll be fine, but I might not be back out there tonight."

"We'll hold down the fort."

Glenn left and Mephisto approached the sickly, shivering girl at his table. She seemed to be coming down already, her energy flagging. God knew how she'd gotten here in her condition. He could picture her wandering the streets of downtown Seattle, clawing at her collar and screaming like a psycho. What might have happened if she hadn't found her way to his place?

"Let me see." He reached for the shining eternity collar, pushing her knotted, lank hair to the side. Her hair used to be her crowning glory, thick and glossy and beautiful, but now it was dull, unwashed. She was trying to sit still but random shudders seized her small frame. "What are you on?" Mephisto asked again, now that she seemed slightly more lucid. "Are you going to go into heart failure on me? What did you take?"

"I don't know. I got it from someone."

"Who?"

She shrugged. "I don't know."

"Okay." He sighed, grasping for patience. "Where were you?"

"Somewhere. I don't remember."

"At home? At a restaurant? At a club?"

"A club. Somewhere."

Mephisto scrubbed a hand over his face. He had to get her collar off before she started yanking at it again. He traced around the smooth edges until he found the tiny depression he was looking for. "Be very still," he said. And then, "Are you sure?"

"Take it off." Her voice was firm. "I'm not his slave anymore."

Fair enough. He lined up the tiny screwdriver with the delicate, almost invisible release. She wasn't the only one shaking. His hands suddenly felt too big, too clumsy for this moment. He poked the sharp tool into the clasp until he managed to wiggle it loose. The collar opened and he eased it from her chafed neck.

She turned to him, breathing hard, her chest rising and falling. "Give it to me."

"No." Not a chance. She'd calmed somewhat, but she was still out of her mind.

"Give it to me!"

"The screaming won't work. You're not getting it until you're down. Here are your choices. Go to the hospital. Go to jail. Spend the night here."

She stood and moved toward the door. "I'm leaving. I'm going home."

He stepped in front of her with a grim look. "I'll repeat your choices one more time. Hospital. Jail. Here."

"You can't keep me here! You don't control me."

"It appears no one controls you. Even you."

"You can't make me stay here against my will. That's kidnapping."

"Okay. Jail then. Hospital will cost too much." Mephisto got out his phone.

"Give me that collar!" She launched herself at him but he held the collar over his head, subduing her with one tight arm around her waist. She flailed, spitting at him. "You're an asshole!"

"Yes, and an abuser. I remember."

"And a criminal!"

"Says the girl who's high on some illegal substance." He pulled her over to the sink and made her drink an entire glass of water, even though most of it ended up on his clothes, and then took her to the bathroom. "Sit down and piss," he said. "And if you dare go anywhere but in the bowl I'll fucking destroy your ass."

She scowled and used the toilet, then stood and defiantly kicked off her thong panties and wisp of a skirt. "Are you going to rape me now?"

"There is nothing on earth I'd find less appealing at the moment. Put your skirt back on."

"Fuck you."

With a sigh, Mephisto picked up her skirt and panties and carried them, along with the resisting woman, into his room. He flung her discarded clothes into a cage in the corner. Then he looked at Molly. "In you go."

"Fuck you!"

"One more time, because I know you're high and stupid right now. Hospital. Jail. Here. Pick your fucking choice."

She kicked him hard in the shin, which fucking hurt, then drew her knee back to aim for his balls. Before she could complete such an ill-advised attack, he forced her into the rectangular cage, shutting the door and locking it while she pounded on the bars. "You're going to be in so much fucking trouble when I call the police," she screeched. "This is kidnapping!"

"This is tough love. I'll let you out when whatever is in your system has worn off."

"I hate you. I hate you!" Bang, bang, bang on the bars. He sat on the edge of the bed and watched to be sure she wouldn't hurt herself. She banged for a minute, two minutes, but then she went still and lay back, and the sobbing started. Wails and sobs and threats of what would happen to him. "I have money, you asshole!" she shrieked. "I'm fucking rich. I'll ruin you!"

Mephisto wondered how much of Clayton's fortune Molly had managed to lose or burn through in the last month and a half. Not too much, he hoped. He shouldn't have left her alone, even though she sent him away. He realized that now.

"I hate you. I hate you. *I hate you.*" Screams turned to whines and whines turned to whimpers and then she was all raged out and there was only her vicious glare. He studied the slim metal circlet between his fingers, remembering better times. She followed him with her eyes as he stood and crossed the room to lay her collar on top of his chest of drawers. Such a beautiful, delicate work of art. He remembered when Clayton had first showed it to him. He'd had it specially made for her.

"It would have killed him to see you this way," Mephisto said. Not to her, because she was in no state to listen. He just said it because it was the dismal truth.

* * * * *

Molly woke to dark blurry lines in front of her face. Bars. She was in jail. She'd figured it would happen eventually. She turned over with a moan to focus on a dark gaze beyond the black lines.

No, not jail. She was in Mephisto's cage.

She'd been here before, in another lifetime. In her old life, which revolted her now. Her hands moved to her neck. Bare. She vaguely remembered Mephisto taking off her collar last night.

A wry voice. "Good morning, starshine." The noise hurt her head.

"Let me out of here. I need a drink."

"Of water, right?"

39

She banged the bars, which hurt her head worse. "Just let me out. I'm sober now."

He came over and knelt by the cage, working the padlock with quick fingers. "Hello, Molly. Nice to see you again."

She lifted her chin and crawled out, struggling to her feet. "What's that supposed to mean?"

"I mean, I haven't seen you in a while. The crazy, insane Molly I used to know. Wait, maybe it's not so nice to see you again. Maybe you barged in here last night high as a kite and screamed at me while you almost took your own head off trying to rip off your collar. Oh yeah, that's what happened."

"Why don't you shut up?" Molly was weaving on her feet. Mephisto grabbed her and led her to his bed, an iron monstrosity with a "bad girl" cage underneath.

"Sit. I'll be back in a minute."

He stalked out, and Molly would have fled if she could have. Giving orders already. That's what men like him always did, how they got off. Just like her Master. She would have torn out of that room, through the dungeon and out to freedom. Freedom from men who liked to boss her and control her. Unfortunately, she could barely stay upright in a sitting position, much less stand. Mephisto returned, holding out two pills and a glass of water.

"What is this?"

"You should have asked that question to someone last night," he said. "It's arsenic. Take it."

Molly's brain shuddered and kicked into gear. Arsenic? No, it wasn't really arsenic. He was being sarcastic, which didn't do much to improve her mood or the pain in her head. She held out her hand for the medicine and took it with a whole glass of water. She was so thirsty. So tired. He reached out to her and she flinched.

"I was just going to take the glass back. Give it to me." She handed it over and flinched again as he reached for her. He shook his head. "Relax, would you? I need to check your neck."

40

He brushed her hair back and traced light fingers just above her collarbone and at her nape. He gave a low whistle. "Jesus. You're black and blue."

She glared at him. "It wouldn't be the first time."

He sat down on the bed beside her, but he didn't touch her again, and he didn't speak anymore, thank God. She gazed over at the cage, wondering what she was doing here. Wondering if she'd come here high on drugs because she subconsciously knew it was the only safe place for her to go. The only place she'd be kept safe from herself, by the only person who wouldn't put up with her shit. Her headache lessened, replaced by this disturbing thought: She wanted to go back in his cage.

She lurched to her feet. "Oh, God."

"What is it?"

"I have to go. I have to go right now. I have to—"

"You're not going anywhere yet."

She reeled over to the low, solid cage and leaned against it. She was so afraid. So confused.

"You want to get back in, don't you?" he asked. "It's okay if you do."

"No, it's not!"

"Why? Because it's disgusting?"

She turned on him. "Because I don't want that. I don't want what I had before. I don't want cages and collars and crawling around and...and subjugating myself, especially not to you."

"Okay." Mephisto held up his hands and smiled. "See? That's how you start a conversation about it. You decide what you don't want. You decide what you do want. You explain it to the person you're in a relationship with."

"I'm not in a relationship with you." Her hands made fists at her sides. *No, you don't want him. No. Stupid slave idiot.* "I don't want a relationship with you. I don't." She sounded so much like she was trying to convince herself. He looked at her like she'd lost leave of her senses.

"Uh, excuse me, but I never said you did. I said 'the person you're in a relationship with.'"

41

"I don't want a relationship with anyone. Especially not you."

He was still giving her the psycho stare. "Okay," he said. "Why don't you come sit down again? Or come with me to the kitchen to get something to eat? Something besides drugs of dubious origin." She hated the way he looked at her, like she was broken. Messed up. Shameful. "I want to ask what you've been up to the last couple months, but I'm afraid of what you'll say." The final dig. Nice.

Molly grumbled and said she wasn't hungry, but a short while later, after a shower and change of clothes from Mephisto's spare room, she was sitting at the table in his gleaming kitchen, which was doubtless cleaned and spit-polished weekly by one of his many adoring slaves. She'd cleaned it too, several times. She'd knelt at his feet and let him feed her, not once, not twice, but for a whole week. She put that memory out of her head, but so many others crowded back to her in vivid detail. Two years had done nothing to dull the memory of her time with him—the good parts and the bad.

He put food in front of her and she ate it mechanically, because in some part of her brain she knew she had to eat or not survive. Since her Mast—Mr. Copela—Clayton had died, she'd gone whole days without eating anything, wondering why she was so hungry while she lay in bed. *Oh, I forgot to eat. Again.*

While she ate, Mephisto plied her with questions. She knew how his whole questioning thing worked. Always casual on the surface, while ruthlessly seeking information underneath. Talking to him sometimes felt like being interrogated, even though he never moved or raised his voice. It was his eyes that stripped her bare. She had no defenses, even now, even as a free, non-kinky person trying to reinvent herself. Under Mephisto's gaze, his quiet questions, she revealed exactly what she meant to hide from him. From everyone. She wasn't reinventing herself at all. She was falling back into the bedlam of her past, which terrified her. *Oh, God help me. What am I going to do?*

"Molly."

She didn't even realize she'd buried her face in her hands. "What?" she asked from between her fingers.

"I can call someone if you like. A counselor. Someone who helps people with grief."

"No."

"I know kink-friendly mental health professionals."

"No, nothing's wrong with me." She dropped her hands to the table and looked off over his shoulder, wishing she could make him understand. "I'm just sad. Confused. I need time."

"I understand that, but I don't think you're dealing with your sadness in an appropriate way."

"Thanks for the newsflash. I know I'm not."

He moved his chair closer to hers. "Where are you going to go when you leave here? What are you going to do?"

Great questions. Molly didn't have any answers. She shrugged. "I don't know."

"I mean, what does your day look like? You wake up, you have breakfast, and then you do...what?"

She scowled. "I usually wake up around three or four in the afternoon, get dressed, go out for a drink, and then...stay out until four A.M. or so."

Mephisto was silent. She swallowed hard and stuck her chin out.

"Partying. I party until 4 A.M. or so."

"Yeah, I figured." He sighed and leaned back in his chair. "And does that make you feel better?"

"Yes. It dulls the pain." She put her face in her hands again. She was so tired. So exhausted from fighting and trying to make her own way in the world, when all she was doing was falling back into bad habits. Hurting herself. She wanted her Master back, to fix things, to tell her what to do. To make her feel better again, to feel safety and contentment instead of this eviscerating grief.

"I miss him so badly," she choked out. "I miss him *so much*."

She felt a touch on her back, just a soft brush of fingers. She turned to Mephisto and buried her face against his arm.

"I didn't mean those things I said about him before. I'm just lost, and angry. I miss him. I feel like I'm going to die."

"I know," Mephisto said softly. "I can see how much you miss him."

"I know he loved me. And I loved him so much. And now...now I just don't see how to go on. I don't know what to do with myself, where to go in my life. I don't want to be anyone else's slave."

"You don't have to be."

"But... But..." She started bawling like an idiot. "I kind of do. I miss being taken care of. I'm so lonely. And so stupid and needy." All the words came spilling out along with the tears soaking Mephisto's shoulder. He put his arms around her and squeezed her, his warmth so familiar and comforting.

"It's not stupid to feel needy. Not right now. Of course you feel needy. Clayton knew you would feel this way, and he worried very much about it. We talked about it many times." He leaned back to brush her damp hair from her eyes. "He knew you very well."

"Why did he leave me?" The question came out a ragged wail, while Molly cried into the wall of Mephisto's chest. "Why? Why, *why?*" No matter how many times she asked it, no reasonable answer was forthcoming. Mephisto offered no reassurances, no platitudes, just a steadily beating heart against her ear. Molly cried until her eyes burned and her lungs hurt and then she fell into a kind of stupor, just drifting, feeling secure and safe for the first time in a long time in the circle of Mephisto's arms.

"I should have been there for you before now," he whispered. "I promised Clay."

Molly sniffled and sat up, rubbing her eyes. "It was my fault. Choices I made." Her lips twisted into a quavery smile. "You should have put me in the bad girl cage last night."

"I might have, if I wasn't so afraid you'd hurt yourself. You scared me. You freaked me out."

She gazed into his eyes, so intent with concern. "I'm sorry, Mephisto. For this craziness. For dragging you into my issues."

"No, I'm glad you dragged me into them. Will you let me help you? Help you find happiness again?"

Any thought of Mephisto and help always triggered confused, guilty feelings in her. She tensed and drew away from him, needing space, but his hands tightened on her.

"No. Not like that. I know you don't want that. Let me help you, no strings attached. Let me help you as a friend."

"How?"

"By bringing a little structure to your life. I understand you're not into fetish anymore, so I won't offer any kind of BDSM dynamic. But I would like to take care of you for a while. Help you get back on track."

Molly knew Mephisto. She knew what his offer meant. "You think I need control. Someone to control me."

He raised a shoulder, tilting his head to the side with a small smile. "Control is such an aggressive word. Let me manage you for a while."

Manage. That was a slightly less loaded word. She dropped her head to the table, thunking her forehead. Mephisto sighed. She looked up again, grabbing her hair in fistfuls.

"Why am I like this?" she moaned. "Why can't I just take care of myself like a normal person?"

"You can. You're here, aren't you? You found your way here even half out of your mind."

"But why?"

"Why is the earth round, Molly? Why is the sky blue? Who the fuck knows why? Who cares? If you need to feel managed to survive for a while, then be managed. Don't break yourself into pieces over it."

"But it's not normal!"

"By whose compass? What scale of normalcy are you judging yourself by? Margaret Kearney's scale? Gloria Steinem's? Dr. Phil's? The only scale you should be using is your own."

"My scale says I'm batshit crazy."

"Mine does too, at the moment. But you've known peace. Give yourself some time to figure out what you crave, what will fulfill you. What will make your world bright again. Accept yourself as you are and don't worry about what anyone else thinks." He leaned close to her, taking her hands, perhaps in some attempt to keep her from twisting her hair out of her head. "You're feeling shame for who you are, and it pains me. These are the same shame-based issues that drove you to become self-destructive before. I don't know where it comes from, but I know it's not good for you."

Shame. The bane of her life. Even now, shame covered her like a cloak. It kicked her between the legs, over and over. She looked down at her hands entwined with Mephisto's, pale white and warm brown fingers interlaced. He gazed into her eyes. "You have nothing to be ashamed of, you know."

"That's because you accept me as I am. Because you understand me."

He took a deep breath as the words she'd said echoed around and around in her head. Clayton, her husband, her Master, her love... He'd begun trying to bring Molly and Mephisto together even before he died. Because of this. Because Mephisto understood her, because he didn't judge her or make her feel shamed and worthless for wanting to live under the dominion of a man.

And because Mephisto was safe.

"Please help me," she said. Her voice cracked and the tears started again, but Mephisto didn't let go of her hands. "I...I don't know yet what I want. I don't know how much control I want."

"Of course you don't. I understand that."

"I can't promise... I can't give you anything yet. I mean, some, but not very much. I just don't know..."

He let go of her hand to stroke her face. His fingers slid through her tears, warm and reassuring. "It's okay not to know. Let's forget about the future and just take care of now. We'll take things slow and keep them nonsexual. I'll only provide the structure, the authority you miss."

"Can you do that?" she asked through tears. "Can people exchange power and have it not be sexual?"

"Sure they can."

"You would do that for me?"

He gazed at her for a long moment. "Molly, I would do almost anything for you. You have to realize that by now. But I'll need you to stay here with me to make this work. You'll be clothed, there won't be any sexual expectations. You'll be taking care of yourself as much as possible, but I still want you here where I can keep track of you."

She tensed. "In the cage?"

"In the guest room." He paused. "Unless you wig out of your brain again, but that better not happen. No drugs, Molly. No alcohol, unless I allow it. This is not negotiable."

Molly blushed under his direct regard. "I can live without that stuff. I'm actually tired of being so out of control."

"Control, management, supervision, whatever. I'm happy to give it to you if it will help. We'll go over to Clayton's today to get whatever you might need to feel at home here. Your clothes and things."

The easy authority in his voice was like a familiar coat wrapping around her. Molly swallowed hard and settled into the security she'd been missing for weeks now.

"Yes, sir," Mephisto provided quietly when she didn't respond.

"Yes, sir," Molly said.

CHAPTER FOUR
MANAGEMENT

Molly stalled at the door to the home she and Clayton had shared. Mephisto figured it would be bad, considering she couldn't meet his gaze. "I'm sure you have things you need to do," she said. "I can pack for myself. I'll take a cab back to your place."

"Open it."

It wasn't a request, but a command. Molly sighed and bent over the lock while Mephisto stared down at the bruises on the back of her neck. They were worst there, since she'd pulled and tugged the collar forward, God knew for how long. Since she'd decided it was shameful and disgusting to be a slave, he supposed. There was no guarantee she wouldn't feel that way again a few hours from now. Tomorrow. Next week. But he'd do what he could to keep that from happening.

The door swung open and Mephisto braced for the mess he expected to find. It was so much worse. He said nothing, only moved into the foyer, studying the trashed living room and the ruined carpet. Mysterious stains decorated the walls.

"I...I might have hosted a few parties."

"I see that."

"I'll clean it up."

He wandered toward the kitchen. The smell hit him long before he got there. Broken dishware littered the floor, and the refrigerator hung open displaying an array of rotting items. In the dining room, a priceless crystal chandelier listed sideways, half torn from the ceiling. Exposed wires stuck out from the base. "Honestly, at this point, it would be best to hire a service to come take care of the cleaning." He sniffed and breathed through his nose. "A service that handles hazardous waste."

How had she been living here in these ruins? She looked around in shock like someone else must have done this. Perhaps she hadn't been sober since the last party. A sobering—pun intended—thought.

"I suppose we have to go to the bedroom to pack your clothes," he said. "Although I'm a little afraid of what I'll find."

The bedroom was ransacked too. "Who was here?" he asked. "Friends of yours?" Molly shrugged as he crossed to her dressing room and lifted the lid of her jewelry box. Empty. "They stole from you."

"They weren't really my friends."

All the jewelry and gifts Clayton had bought his pretty princess. Gone. Mephisto felt rage for a moment, at her "friends," at Molly for being so spoiled and careless, but in a way it was natural consequences. He shut the lid of the box and turned to her. "Okay. Suitcases. Clothes. Whatever you need to bring to my place."

She started to pack, looking a little shell-shocked.

Let her be shell-shocked. She should be. He certainly was. She didn't pack much, and then he went around the house with her picking up anything of value that was left. "Where is the violin?" he asked.

Molly flinched, and then she lied to his face. "I don't know."

His expression hardened. "Lies are not okay with me. Ever."

Molly went back into the bedroom and knelt beside the bed. She stuck her hands underneath and pulled out an open case. The velvet inside was damaged. So was the violin. Strings stuck out every which way and part of the body was crushed.

"I tried to smash it." She buried her face in her hands. "I tried to destroy it."

Mephisto wasn't angry at anything anymore, just really sad for her. "Why?"

"Because I hated it. Because I was never good enough." She looked over at him, her eyes windows to the pain inside her. "This is your fault."

He raised his eyebrows. "Did I smash it?"

"No. You brought it into my life."

You brought him *into my life.* That was what Mephisto heard. He leaned over her, closed the violin case and stowed it under his arm. "We'll try to get it repaired. I'll ask around and see if it's possible." He started out of the room, only to stop by the door. He nudged a half-burned box, turning it over. Shards of singed leather tumbled out, along with a very recognizable chastity shield and buckle. He turned to Molly, one eyebrow raised.

She shifted on her feet. "I tried to burn it...after I shredded it with a pair of scissors."

"You still couldn't kill it though, could you? It will forever haunt your dreams."

She gave him a sour smile. "I'm glad you find it funny. I didn't, you know. Wearing that sadistic contraption for a week, not being permitted to orgasm."

"I never found it funny in the least. I thought it was a wonderful exercise for you. And for me. Did your Master ever use it on you after you came home?"

She shook her head. "I mean, a few times he put it on, to punish me, but I think the sight of me in chastity turned him on too much. He always ended up taking it off a few hours later so he could fuck me."

Mephisto chuckled. "And he let you come, of course."

She shrugged. "It was what he liked."

Mephisto kicked the box, knowing her words for the truth. Clayton lived to drive his slave wild. Mephisto had enjoyed driving her wild too, that week they shared. His methods and Clayton's were just different. "It wasn't the chastity belt that prevented your orgasms, you know," he said. "It was me. You still could have had them. Eventually, you would have found a way. Or you would have if you hadn't been such an exemplary slave."

Past tense. Molly looked so mournful. It would probably be best to get her out of this place. He took her out to lunch and then back to his private residence at Club Mephisto, where they worked together to set her up in the extra room. It was dark in there—no window—but comfortable. Until he was sure she wasn't going to continue taking narcotics, he felt better not having a window in her room. When that was done, he sat her down across from him at his desk out by the dungeon.

"Okay, I've been thinking about expectations for you. I think you lack structure, some sense of purpose, so I'd like to assign you tasks I'll expect you to do every day. As we agreed, they won't be sexual, but they will be required."

Molly nodded, then thought a moment. "I don't want to work in the club. And I don't want to be your housekeeper."

He gave her a look. "Toppy, aren't we?"

"I don't want to be a service slave. I know a lot of subs get off on domestic service, but I'm not into that. You said you would help me manage my life, not make me do stuff I don't want to do."

"Did I say anything about you doing housework for me? Or even being my slave?"

She blushed. "No, sir."

"My only concern is that if you have too much time on your hands you'll find questionable ways to spend it. I'm basing this on your past behavior. Do you think I'm wrong?"

She shook her head. He stared at her until she eked out a "No, sir."

"Here's what I want. Every morning, I'd like you to get yourself out of bed and spend at least two hours doing something to help another person. Anyone. Your choice. Then I want you to spend at least two hours every afternoon doing something to improve yourself. Again, the activity is your choice. All I ask is that you report to me every evening at dinner what you did."

"What happens if I don't?"

"You're out on your ass. No second chances. This will be our arrangement for now, until you get your life back together and decide what you want to do next. Fair enough?"

She was quiet a long moment. Then she said, "I think Clayton would have liked this. You helping me this way. You're so much like him sometimes." Her voice cut off in a little choke.

Let me be what Clayton was to you, then. He didn't say it aloud. It wasn't the time to confront her with that. *When you're ready, Molly. I'll wait.* She quickly composed herself, and he made his own voice firm and businesslike. "So, do you agree or not? I want us to be clear about everything. About what's expected of you and what you expect of me."

She nodded. "Yes, sir. It's clear." He heard the relief in her voice. He thought it had probably been a while since things looked clear to her. The rest of it he could figure out. He wouldn't be as controlling and heavy-handed as Clayton, but he'd control her enough to comfort her. He'd give her occasional orders to keep her engaged, to give her a sense of protection. He'd give her a few light responsibilities around the house to earn her keep.

That night, he also gave her a bedtime, and she didn't fight it. When the hour rolled around Mephisto locked her in her room, with her consent, of course. Her room became then, essentially, a cage, with walls instead of bars.

He, too, would be a cage for her. He hoped it would help. He hoped it would be enough.

* * * * *

Molly settled comfortably into Mephisto's care, not that it was easy. When did he ever make things easy? Finding ways to help others, for instance, was a terrifying experience. She'd been focused so long on serving only one person, she'd never really thought about all the other people in the world who needed help, and all the countless types of help they needed.

The first day, she walked around opening doors for people, and picking up litter on the street. As she did, she watched people. Club Mephisto wasn't in a terrible part of town, but it wasn't in the most affluent area either. She saw a lot of people who looked troubled, but she was too shy to ask how she could help. Mephisto acknowledged her efforts, but encouraged her to be more proactive the next day. Proactive. What a concept. Again, the only thing she'd ever been proactive about was anticipating her Master's wants and needs.

Mephisto pointed her to websites listing non-profit organizations in the area. She made some calls and met some people, and found right away that there was always something to do. Molly was hands-on in the beginning. She liked working on projects, helping people directly, but she knew there was more she could do. She started using some of Clayton's money. That involved meetings with his financial planners, but the money was there, earmarked for charity. It had to be given away for tax purposes. She wasn't sure about all the details of it, but the amount he had donated yearly to charity took her breath away. Now that she was working "down in the trenches," as one of her new friends said, she understood the importance of carrying on his legacy.

The afternoons were more difficult. She couldn't really concentrate on improving herself until she fixed all the things she'd messed up during her wild few weeks. Mephisto agreed, and directed her to go to a doctor first, to be sure she hadn't done anything to her health during her month-long bender. He required STD testing too, which embarrassed her. But it was a relief to learn she'd managed to stay clean. Honestly, she'd been so out of her mind she couldn't remember if she'd fucked anyone or not. Humiliating.

When her personal health was all squared away, the next step was putting Clayton's house back to rights. She cleaned and polished every wall, floor, and surface, and hired people to repair any damage she couldn't. She sorted through Clayton's things, donating nearly everything to charity. All his thousand dollar suits, his designer shoes. His books, his electronics, crying the whole while. His family took his cars and watches, and other extremely valuable things she didn't want.

Molly kept some things too. A belt she knew well, a pair of cufflinks, a delicate silver leash. His wedding ring and his pillow. It still smelled faintly of him. She put it in an airtight bag in her closet at Mephisto's place, to hug sometimes when she missed him badly. She couldn't bear to sleep on it at night. When Mephisto returned her old collar she slipped it down inside the pillowcase. That too she couldn't bear to look at or wear, although she kept on her wedding rings.

Yes, she missed her old Master. She wasn't angry at him anymore, or at herself. She was simply unsettled, lonely, and unsure what to do next. When Clayton's house was empty and clean she locked it up. She couldn't let it go, nor could she rent it out to strangers. Later. She'd decide what to do later. With that squared away, self-improvement began in earnest. She walked to the library and read books about relationships and meditation, about gardening and health, and strangely, child rearing, although her old Master had fixed her so she could never have kids. She told Mephisto every evening about what she'd read. He'd ask her such probing questions that each day she'd read more carefully than the day before.

Other days she exercised, or got her nails done. She shopped for clothes, because she had to wear them every day now, even when she was home with Mephisto. *Non-sexual. For now.* Sex wasn't even distantly in her thoughts most of the time, until it intruded in an uneasy, powerful pang, usually when Mephisto was close to her, or looked at her a certain direct way. Authority turned her on, no matter when or how she encountered it. Those moments of sexual awareness always took her by surprise and left her feeling unsettled.

She took yoga classes and some computer classes at the community college. One day she went to the cell phone store because Mephisto ordered her to join the living and set herself up with a smart phone. She learned how to text and how to surf online and even how to send emails to Mephisto from her phone, keeping him informed of her whereabouts throughout each day. Mephisto returned her violin, restored and in a new velvet-lined case. He urged her to start back to her lessons, but she hid the instrument under the bed.

Luckily, he didn't require her to do everything he suggested. Still, there wasn't a moment she didn't feel he was looking out for her, and it gave her so much strength. She knew she should have been strong enough to take care of herself without reporting to him, without him standing over her, but she wasn't, and that was just the way it was. She could blame daddy, she could blame mommy. She could blame any number of things, but by now she understood that changed nothing. As Mephisto said, Who the fuck knew why? Who cared?

Mentally, Mephisto was all over her, engaging her, demanding her ideas and thoughts—but he never touched her. He didn't fondle her or caress her in passing. He didn't hug her or "accidentally" brush against her, or do anything else to make her feel physically imposed upon. Still, sometimes the memory of their past and his blatant sexual charisma invaded her mind and she almost wished he would touch her, even if the idea scared her to death. When he went out into the club to work, she never went.

Three months passed. Four. Eventually, she stopped keeping her head down and started feeling like part of humanity again. She became part of a new world where she accomplished things, where she helped people and made them smile. Men she worked with started to notice her, even flirt with her. Nice men. Normal men. Men on the street would turn and look at her and she'd feel conflicting feelings of attraction and fear.

Molly started eating lunch now and again in a neighborhood diner, mostly to study the lunch crowd, soak in the real world. Some businessmen were always there, reminding her vaguely of her Master. Today a group of delivery guys clustered around a table nearby, talking and laughing. Did any of them have slaves? Doubtful. One of them was giving her the flirty eyes. He was young. Handsome. Fresh-faced, with scruffy brown hair, a broad smile and a great laugh when his friends cracked jokes. He had that confident energy she was always attracted to. She found herself wondering what he would be like in bed.

Molly frowned and looked down. Ridiculous, to salivate over him. He looked pretty buff in his brown shorts and UPS shirt though. She cast around for any memory of urban legends about delivery guys and perversity. Hmm. Nothing there.

He caught her looking at him, and she dropped her eyes to her BLT. A minute later she looked up again. He was just so...lively. He was *sunny*. He had to know by now she was peeking at him. She forced herself to look elsewhere, to gaze around the room. A mother wrangled a toddler in the corner, while a group of college students huddled over their smart phones in a booth. Two older men, a father and son from the looks of them, argued at the table behind hers. She should have brought a book. She had nothing to do but keep looking at the smiling man. He wasn't her physical type. *He's no Mephisto*, she thought.

Maybe that was why the guy fascinated her so much. He wasn't imposing like Mephisto. He wasn't brooding or studying her like some puzzle he was trying to figure out. He didn't have an ounce of dominance on the surface, and she doubted he had much underneath. He was still sexy in a wholesome, normal type way.

He caught her eyes again. Her face burned as she dropped her gaze to the tabletop and stared at the lettuce scattered over her plate. How long since she'd known anyone outside the BDSM universe? How long since she'd had a friend, just some normal person she knew, someone to laugh and be natural with? There was Mephisto, but he'd always been more protector than friend. There was Mrs. Jernigan... No. Not a friend. Mrs. Bobo, the woman who'd come to do her waxing? Ugh, she'd been an enemy, the sadistic bitch. Molly had spent time with Master's sisters, but she wouldn't consider them friends by a long shot.

Molly wasn't even sure she knew how to have a friend anymore, and that idea really troubled her.

"Hey. Why so sad? Not enough tomato?"

Molly's head shot up, and there he was, sitting down across from her. She clasped her hands in her lap. "What?"

"They're stingy with the tomatoes here, huh? I always get the BLT too. But there are never. enough. tomatoes."

Molly looked down at her plate. "I— I didn't notice. I don't know." Brilliant. She was a scintillating conversationalist. Not. His easy smile and flirtation suddenly saddened her, and she didn't know why. Because she couldn't keep up, maybe. Because he would definitely find her weird. His eyes were blue, the same blue her Master's had been.

He leaned closer. "You look so down. What's wrong? I think you need a piece of pie." Molly gaped at him. "Have some pie with me. You can't have pie and stay sad."

That was a lie, but Molly didn't have the heart to call him on it. She cast about instead for something cute to say in response to his suave banter. "Um. Okay. If you buy."

She couldn't meet his eyes now, not with him so close, but she stared at his smile as it widened. Clean, straight teeth. Sensual lips. "Of course I'll buy," he said. "Cherry or apple?"

"Cherry."

He went to the counter. His friends ribbed him, but he ignored them and returned a couple minutes later with some pieces of pie and some forks. He'd chosen cherry too. Molly took a drink of water and gave him a belated thank you. He was already tearing into his piece. This restaurant had the best pie. Flaky, oozing with fresh filling that was obviously homemade, not pulled out of some freezer. They were like the pies Master's cook used to bake.

"My name's Eliot," he said. "I know, it's awful."

Molly heart hammered with nerves, but she forced herself to smile at him. For a moment she considered giving him a false name in return, but why? She wasn't doing anything wrong, and he wasn't dangerous. He was a sweet, flirty delivery guy who'd just bought her some pie to cheer her up.

"My name's Molly."

"Fighting with hubby?"

"What?"

He nodded down at her hands on the table. "You're twisting your wedding rings and you seem upset. Nice diamond, by the way," he said, eying her engagement setting. She put her hands back in her lap. "Thought maybe you were on the outs with your husband."

"My husband died." God, almost half a year ago. Had it been that long?

Eliot looked stricken. "I'm sorry. You have a good reason to be upset then, and here I'm buying you pie like an idiot."

Molly smiled and took another bite. "It's really good pie."

She wanted another of his easy grins, but his face was different now. Not pitying. That would have irritated her. Just a little more gravity in his gaze. "How long were you married to him?"

"Eight years." *I was his slave. He kept me like a piece of property. I loved it.* She choked a little on the bite in her mouth, and washed it down with a big drink of water. "I miss him. I feel like I lost a little of who I am since he left. Well, a lot of who I am. Or who I was." She waved a hand. "I don't know." How weird, to be spilling out all this stuff to a perfect stranger, but now that she'd started she couldn't seem to stop. "I feel like I'm in this weird Neverland between lives. I feel lost." She shut her mouth. She tasted cherries and misery on her tongue. She didn't want this. She wanted his brightness, not her sob stories. "Are you married?" she asked to change the subject.

He laughed. "Not even close. Although my mother wants me to get married."

"But you're too much of a flirt to settle down," Molly guessed.

He gave her a look of feigned outrage. "Me, a flirt?"

"Worse than a flirt, I bet."

He laughed then, and Molly trembled a little inside. With fear, with power. With the novelty of a man's appreciative laugh. "Look, I don't buy pie for every woman I meet," he said.

It was her turn to laugh. "Only the sad ones."

"Yes, only the sad ones. So I can see them smile."

Not flirting now. Sincerity. Such kind sincerity. Their eyes met, Molly's forkful of pie arrested halfway to her lips. She'd smiled more in the last five minutes than the whole previous week. "It feels good to smile," she said. "It really feels good. So thanks."

He seemed embarrassed now. He tucked into his pie with renewed vigor. "So what do you do, Molly? You work?"

"No. Well..." She thought a moment. "I guess I'm searching for a position right now. Deciding what to do with my life."

"I hope you're okay since...since your husband died."

"Oh, I'm fine. He left me with plenty to get by," she said, in gross, gross understatement. "But I need to figure out where I go from here." She didn't want to tell Eliot the truth, with his earnest kindness and helpfulness, that she had more in her slush account than he'd probably make in a lifetime, and untold more tied up in investments and real estate.

"Well," he said, scraping his fork across his plate, "you should definitely take the time now to consider your options. This has got to feel like a crazy time."

"Yes, it does." She couldn't eat anymore. She was full. She could see across the diner that Eliot's friends were squaring their bills and preparing to leave. "Still, pie helps," she said.

"Pie helps everything." He looked over his shoulder. "Well, I have to go. It was a pleasure meeting you. Maybe I'll see you here some time again."

She nodded. It took so little time to scarf down a piece of pie. Yes, maybe she'd see him again. Did she want to? She felt conflicted. He started to leave but then came back toward her table.

"Listen, is there a day you're usually here?"

"I'm usually here on Fridays. Around noon." The lie came out so easily. Eliot grinned.

"Cool. Maybe I'll see you then."

She watched him leave. He wasn't her type, really. He was young, so much younger than her. Maybe twenty-two or twenty-three, for God's sake, and she was thirty. Maybe next Friday at noon she'd be miles away from here, doing something reasonable. She hoped so. But she doubted it. She really, really adored his smile.

CHAPTER FIVE
A NEW FRIEND

Mephisto watched Molly across the table from under his lids. She was fidgety, nervous. Something had happened. He was sure of it, but he wouldn't pry. She'd been doing so well, getting back out into the world, staying busy doing healthy rather than unhealthy things.

These nightly mealtimes were a ritual he was becoming alarmingly attached to. And disturbed by. The physical pull to her was excruciating, but the emotional pull even more so. He wanted to shelter her. He wanted to improve her. God, he wanted to touch her. By this point he was losing his mind a little.

He wanted to fuck her raw.

Don't. Don't think about her that way. He couldn't let himself dwell on those kinds of thoughts or they'd start to manifest in the way he treated her. He'd start trying to manipulate her, ease her along a continuum so she was giving him what he wanted before she even realized what was up. He could do it every bit as handily as Clayton and he knew it, so he guarded against it. He'd promised Clayton to help her find the life *she* wanted. Molly. Her choice, not his.

But this was hell. Trying to help her find independence, self-actualization, when it only distanced her more from him and any possibility of them ever being together. So be it. He didn't want to manipulate her into his service and spend every minute of every scene feeling guilt for the pleasure she brought him. If she came to him—if she ever came to him—it would be with full knowledge, free will, and want. *God, Molly, want me. Damn you.*

Molly was making a mess of the Pad Thai on her plate. Mephisto tried to distract himself from the sight of her delicate fingers, her pursed lips. It was Friday night. He had to be thinking about the club. Friday night was one of Club Mephisto's busiest nights and the staff would be arriving soon. Molly hid away on club nights, stayed in her room until Mephisto locked the door around two-thirty in the morning, after he checked on her. Then he'd fall into bed, exhausted. Sometimes, before Molly, he'd allow a slave to serve him. Now he slept alone.

"Are you coming to the club tonight?" he asked when she pushed her plate away. He wanted her to understand the option was there. If she wanted to start playing again, even with someone other than him, he wanted her to understand it was okay. There weren't many unattached doms of Clayton's caliber at Club Mephisto. Most were snapped up by savvy submissives within a few weeks, but there were a few worthy ones who were still looking. If Molly wanted to get back into the fray by playing with them, it was fine with him.

Liar. Okay, not fine with him. But if she wanted to...

To his relief, she gave her usual shrug. "I don't think so."

"You could, you know. Even to watch. Even to hang out."

She bit her lip and shook her head. "No. Not yet."

Not yet. Interesting. A step beyond her usual flat no.

"It's okay. Whenever you want to," he persisted. "If you want to get back into the scene..."

"I met someone." She looked up at him, then down again at her plate. Mephisto waited for more, but nothing came.

"You met who?"

She shrugged. Talking to Molly could be a frustrating study in shrugs and shuttered facial expressions. He longed to be able to snap at her to sit up straight and answer clearly. He drew in a breath and let it out.

"You met someone at the Family Center today? Or at the gym?"

"I went to lunch at Mack's Diner. I met someone there. A guy."

Mephisto waited. Stared. Felt a frisson of jealous alarm spread wide in his chest. If Molly had met someone who interested her, he would owe it to Clayton to fan the flame. Ugh.

"What kind of guy?" Mephisto felt himself boxed into the dad role, drawing her out about a new suitor. "Nice guy, I guess?"

She smiled. "Nice? What does that mean? He was some delivery guy on a lunch break. But he was...yeah. Nice. He bought me some pie. I talked to him a little about Clayton."

Mephisto's eyes went wide. "What about Clayton? Everything about Clayton?"

"No, just that he died."

"You didn't tell him who he was? Who you are? You have to be careful telling strange guys about your money."

"I didn't tell him anything, except that my husband died." She put her shoulders back in a gesture of annoyance. "Anyway, it wasn't like that. Like he was honing in on me with some ulterior motive. He was just a friendly person. We ate pie and chatted for like, five minutes."

"You can eat pie with whoever you want. Just be careful." Okay, Mephisto had to back off, regroup. Jealous, petty anger coated all his words. "I think... I think it's great that you met a friendly guy who bought you some pie." There were long minutes of silence, his fork clinking on his plate.

Molly toyed with her napkin. "He was... I don't know. Really young though."

"Kinky."

"I don't think so."

Mephisto chuckled. "No, I meant it's kinky that you're going after a younger guy. But he's not kinky, you don't think?"

Another shrug. God, to be able to forbid those shrugs, and punish every one of them. They'd be in the dungeon for a week. "Who knows?"

Molly said. "I don't think you can always tell, but my dom radar is pretty developed and it didn't go off. Still, it was nice to talk to someone normal. To make a friend."

In other words, Mephisto wasn't normal. Or her friend, in her eyes. He suddenly hated this Pie Casanova with a vengeance. He forced approving words from his lips. "I'm happy for you, Molly. Sounds like it was a good day. Do you think you'll meet with him again?"

"I don't know."

She was lying to him. Mephisto stood abruptly, feeling rage which he could not, *could not* give voice to. "Help me clean up the kitchen, please. It's almost time for the club to open." It took everything he had to keep the words calm and casual.

"Yes, sir."

They cleaned up in silence. Mephisto was glad. He didn't want to think of chatty things to say when he was all tied in knots. He should be happy for her. If she met some vanilla delivery guy who bought her pie, and that kind of stuff made her happy now, that's what Mephisto wanted for her. It just wasn't what he wanted for himself. Why did relationships have to be about two people? Why couldn't he just force Molly to be his slave? Make her kneel at his feet, serve him, suck his cock and do whatever other perverse sexual acts he desired? The necessity of consent made everything so goddamn complicated. He chuckled softly at that thought.

"What?" Molly asked, turning to him. "What are you laughing about?"

"Nothing," Mephisto said. "What kind of pie was it?"

Molly gave him a look. "Cherry."

Cherry. Of course.

* * * * *

Molly tried to put Eliot out of her mind, but he crept back in at the least opportune moments. She was being so stupid. It was so stupid to get obsessed over someone just because she liked his looks. Because he was nice to her. Still, she took twice as long to get dressed and ready on Friday as she usually did, to the point where the other volunteers at the Family Center noticed and asked if she had a hot date. They were teasing her, sweet natured teasing, but she felt mortified. If they noticed, then Eliot would, and he would know...

Know what? That she was interested in him? Why was that so bad? Why was she so scared?

She dragged her feet all the way down the street to the diner, thinking every moment that she still had time to turn around and flee. She also thought he might not show up at all. That would be embarrassing after the way she'd built this up in her head. It wasn't like they'd set up an official date. She thought back to their parting conversation. *I'm usually here on Fridays. Around noon.*

Cool. Maybe I'll see you then.

Oh God, maybe he'd be there but not actually talk to her. He'd nudge his work buddies. "Look, she actually came back." All of them would give her the side eye and snicker and she'd feel that shame again, kicking her, punching her. She stopped on the sidewalk a few steps from the door, her hands in fists. She couldn't bear something like that. She was too afraid to even try this, this friendly, nice relationship, because a betrayal from a nice person was so much worse than a betrayal from someone you knew you couldn't trust.

Molly spun and fled headfirst into a brick wall. No, not a brick wall. A solid, smiling man in a brown UPS uniform. He steadied her with his hands.

"Good golly, Miss Molly. How are you?"

She ducked her head, trying to pull herself together. *Act normal.* She stepped back and forced a laugh. "I'm fine. Sorry. I thought maybe I forgot something back at—where I work—but now I remember I didn't."

"Oh, you got a job!" He looked overjoyed for her. "Where?"

"The Family Center around the corner. I work there part time." It wasn't a total lie. She pointed at his uniform. "I guess you still work for UPS."

"Packages gotta get delivered. You know how it is." There was the smile, radiant and miraculously free of judgment. "You want to get some lunch? Do you have time?"

She nodded and walked with him into the diner. "So, where are your friends?"

He made a face. "They're not my friends, exactly. I work with them. They didn't want to come here today and I didn't argue. It's nice to have a break from them, not that they aren't great guys. They just... When you're around the same people all the time, they start to grate on you."

They sat at a table in the corner, amidst the usual mixed crowd. He leaned close as she stared down at her menu. "You look nice."

They were just casual words, a polite comment, but she felt ridiculously pleased.

"So what do you do at the Family Center? Are you a counselor? A nurse?"

"Oh, God, no. I just help with filing and talk to the people who come in. A lot of them are...nervous." A lot of them were desperate and borderline hysterical, but it seemed too dramatic to tell him that. Just that morning, she'd sat with a bruised and battered woman while the people at the Center helped her get a restraining order against her husband. What was the most dramatic thing that happened down at the UPS hub? A misdirected package? Molly shrugged and made little rips in the edges of her napkin. "Actually, I'm only volunteering there for now. I've been volunteering at a lot of different places, trying to figure out where I belong. What I want to do now." God, why did she keep repeating that like an idiot?

"Well, what did you do before he died?" Eliot asked.

"I stayed at home. I guess I really didn't do anything." *Except wear his collar for eight years, and try to be perfect for him.*

"So, you were one of those trophy wives, huh?" Eliot raised a brow and smiled at her over his menu.

Molly coughed. "Uh. Not exactly. Sort of. My M— My husband was older, yes." She'd come so close to slipping up and calling him her Master in front of Eliot. "He was older, but I didn't marry him for money or security or anything. I loved him. I didn't just shop and soak in the tub and eat bon bons."

"You just described my dream life."

Molly burst out laughing as the waitress came by to take their orders. They both ordered BLTs, and Eliot asked for extra tomato, winking at Molly, so she laughed again as the waitress bustled away. He ran a hand through his chestnut mop of hair and flashed her another of his wonderful smiles.

"I would make a great trophy husband for some rich woman. What do you think? Know any rich old ladies looking for some young lovin'?"

Molly almost choked on her sandwich. "If I meet any rich old ladies I'll be sure to put in a word for you. But we don't get a lot of them at the Family Center."

They talked and laughed for almost an hour over BLTs and sodas and cherry pie. Eliot kept her in stitches telling stories about his oddball co-workers and his large, hilariously dysfunctional family. She found out he was twenty-four, and that he was working to earn money to finish a law degree he'd started a couple years back. She could see him as a lawyer. He had the charisma for it, and he seemed really sharp.

"I have an Environmental Studies degree," she blurted out. "A lot of my friends moved into Environmental Law in college."

"Oh yeah, that's a big area now. Where'd you go to school?"

"Indiana University. They have some great programs."

Eliot folded his arms and leaned on the table, looking confused. "So why don't you get back into that? If that's what you have a degree in?"

"That was another lifetime. It feels like it anyway. I'm not that person anymore."

"Well, what person are you?"

Molly paused, then shook her head. "I don't know. I just know..." She looked up at Eliot with a shy smile. "I just know the pie here is really good. And the conversation."

His gaze met hers and held it. "Next Friday then? Or...maybe I could call you sometime this week. Maybe we could do something else. Dinner and a movie?"

Molly blinked. "I— Well—"

"Sorry. Didn't mean to freak you out. We get along though, don't we?" His voice dropped a half-octave. "And I am getting kind of addicted to your laughter."

"It's just that I'm not an old, rich sugar mama."

Eliot chuckled. "See? I must really like you then."

Molly gave him her number, feeling excitement but surprise too. Dinner and a movie? It had only been a few months since Clayton died, since she thought her life was over. In a thousand years, she wouldn't have foreseen this. A chance meeting at a diner, and now dinner and a movie.

But Mephisto...

Why did it feel like she was cheating on two men? Her late Master, and Mephisto too? She could tell Mephisto had been less than thrilled to learn about Eliot. She wondered what her Master would have made of him. Was Eliot someone he would have chosen for Molly to be with next?

No, your Master would have chosen Mephisto. Mephisto, who wasn't at all the dinner-and-a-movie type.

Molly pushed that thought out of her brain, but it constantly returned, bringing guilt and confusion over the long weekend. Mephisto left her alone and she hid out in her room. Hid from him, hid from the club activities that still compelled her. The truth was, Molly did still feel an enduring draw to Mephisto. She was just afraid to take any step that would solidify it, because she knew, somehow, that if she gave herself to Mephisto it would be for life. Irreversible. The power they created together was just too strong. A forest fire, rather than a nice fireplace glow. She wanted the fireplace. Calm, normalcy. Maybe even...kids.

She'd been thinking a lot lately about children. She interacted with a lot of children at the Center, at the Women's Clinic, at the homeless shelters and schools, all the places she volunteered her time. There were children everywhere and more and more they touched her heart and made her long for one of her own. It didn't matter. Her Master had her tubes tied after she begged him to, after she'd lost a baby and been in the hospital, unable to serve him. The loss of herself, the loss of control had terrified her. Back then she'd been haunted by the idea that she might have another baby, one that grew heavy in her womb and was actually born. She'd worried about what that might do to her and her Master's dynamic. She'd cried and pleaded and petitioned to be sterilized, even though she knew it was selfish. If Master had wanted a baby, she would have given him one, but he'd claimed not to want one either.

But she grieved now for the baby she lost, the baby that was her and her Master united in one being, gone now, all gone. She grieved for the future babies she might have had. It was silly, but she did. She looked around online and learned that certain types of tubal ligation could be reversed, but it wasn't a sure thing. There was in vitro fertilization. Adoption. She decided she deserved to be childless and put it out of her mind, but like her thoughts of Mephisto, the thoughts of children kept coming back.

If only she could numb all the thoughts and confusion crowding her brain. She wanted Mephisto's reassurance, his strength. It was Saturday night, though, and he was busy with the club. She could go out there into the play dungeon. Just to see him...

Against her better judgment, Molly dressed in some black jeans and a tee, put on some lipstick. No one would mistake her for someone who'd come to play, but she could at least move through the club unobtrusively and see what Mephisto was up to. He often encouraged her to visit the club. She hadn't because...because...

Because she didn't want to see him playing with someone else. Silly, when she refused to have him.

She inched in through the side door, feeling scared, vulnerable, and excited all at once. She was over in the farthest corner of the club, by Mephisto's office, beside the bar, but the sounds and smells reached her there as well as anywhere in the club. Moans, sighs, screams and laughter. A rhythmic sound of impact that echoed in pulse beats right between her legs. It had been so long since she played, since she'd been around anyone doing BDSM, but her body remembered like it was yesterday.

She searched for Mephisto and saw him across the room, his tall stature, muscular body, and wild dreadlocks unmistakable. He was shirtless, his tight dark jeans hugging his taut hips and accentuating his powerful thighs. He was playing with two girls and another guy. One of the girls was in bondage, legs spread, arms outstretched, on a sex swing. The other girl and the guy were playing with her, teasing her, hurting her with a tawse and molesting her as she writhed in her bonds.

She looked ecstatic.

Subspace. Mephisto was watching, enjoying the scene. He assisted the players and seemed to be offering suggestions to the restrained girl's partners—Molly could tell by that familiar gleam in his eyes. She'd been the victim of his clever, brutal sadism many times, and enjoyed every second of it. She buried her face in her hands, too jealous to watch any more. No matter what she told herself, no matter how she avoided the issue, she wanted him so badly. He was the perfect combination of nurturing, cruel, and sexy, that rare, heady mixture that drove her wild. Very few men had it. Her Master had it. Mephisto had it in spades.

"What's the matter?" Molly looked up into the dark, concerned gaze of her protector. She couldn't answer, could only stare at him and think how much he aroused her and scared her at the same time. "I looked over and saw you with your head in your hands," he said. "I thought you were crying."

She shook her head and tried to think of something, anything to reply. "No, I was just watching."

His face softened. "You don't have to hide in the corner. Come out into the play space."

"No, I can't. I don't... I don't belong here anymore. People will..."

"What? Grab you? Force you to play when you don't want to?"

"They'll know I don't belong here."

Mephisto rolled his eyes. "You came here for years. Everybody knows you. Everyone would be thrilled to see you."

"That's just it. They know the old me."

Mephisto took her elbow and led her into the shadows behind the bar. "The old you? The disgusting, slavey you? These are your people, Molly."

"I'm just saying, I'm not like them anymore." She peered out into the dungeon. It was familiar and yet so scary to her. Sinister. With a start, she realized it was the pull to participate that scared her the most. Mephisto touched her face, stroked a finger down her cheek.

"Come play. Just a little? With me?"

She shook her head, but she knew he could see the war in her face, in her mind. He wouldn't have asked otherwise. "No," she said loudly, like she could convince herself. "No, I don't want to."

"I think you do."

He stepped closer, one hand a feather touch at her waist. "Nothing sexual. You wouldn't even have to take off your clothes."

She stared at his broad, bronze chest, at the tense set of his jaw. "No," she lied. "I don't want it."

"Molly..."

"I don't."

"Look at me."

She couldn't. She couldn't possibly. Screams and moans from the play space resonated in the tips of her breasts and her pelvis, taunting her. "I have to go." He caught her arm and held it. "Let me go," she repeated, pulling away.

"Go. Run then. Why did you even come out here?"

To see you. She rubbed her forehead. "I don't know. I don't know why I did." She looked up at him, her eyes pleading, saying what her voice could not.

He inclined his head to hers and brushed his lips against her temple. His hands sought hers, cool and enveloping. "I don't know how to help you. I don't understand what's going on in your mind. Talk to me."

"I can't. I can't!" She pushed him away and ran, just as he'd told her to, ran back to her room and shut the door. It flew open a moment later.

"What?" he yelled. He spread his arms wide, his features pinched in frustration. "What do you need?"

"Just go," she spat back. "Go back to one of your many slaves. Don't let me keep you."

"Oh, my 'many slaves.' You sound jealous, kitten."

His old nickname for her hit her like a slap upside the head. "I'm not jealous."

"Tell me what you need. Tell me what you want and I'll give it to you."

I don't want to have what I want. I don't want the things I need. Because I really think I need you. Mephisto knew. He was trying to get her to admit it to herself, but that would mean confessing that she hadn't changed at all since her Master's death, that she was still the wanton, submissive sex doll her Master had enjoyed so much. She buried her hands in her hair and covered her ears. "Please just leave me alone."

He crossed to her, taking her arms in a firm grip that came really close to hurting. But not quite.

"Don't act like nothing's going on here," he said in a low, accusing voice. "Jesus. It makes me furious."

She pulled away from him, using the last reserves of her assertiveness. "What are you going to do? Punish me? Spank me? Put me into chastity until I tell you what you want to hear?"

"I think it would help you if I did." He released her and stepped back. "Is all of this because I keep other slaves? Because you think I don't want you? That they're more important to me than you are?"

Molly sucked in a deep breath. "You can do what you want with whoever you want. I don't care."

"Why don't we keep it real, Molly? You want me. You want *us*. You're fighting it and I don't understand why. Because of this new guy you met? What's his name again? Idiot?"

"Eliot!" she cried. "Don't mock him. He's nice. He's a nice, normal guy, not like you, with your slaves and sex club and all your partners who'll come on a dime and do whatever you want at a word from you—"

"Yes, that's my lifestyle. That's been my lifestyle since long before I met you."

"I don't want that. I wouldn't want that. When I was with my Master, I was..." Her voice broke. She turned away from him, clasping her hands to her chest. "I was special to him." God, it hurt. Molly wanted Mephisto so badly, but not as one of his harem, his umpteen service slaves to be called upon when he wanted her, or ignored when he wanted another flavor for the day. "I wouldn't want to be yours if I couldn't be special to you. If I couldn't be your only one. I know that doesn't sound very submissive, but there you go." She finished with an undignified sniffle.

Mephisto sighed. "Maybe you haven't noticed that I haven't been with anyone since you moved into my guest room. This is the room where my slaves used to stay."

"I'm sorry I'm interfering in your sex life," she said bitterly. "Sorry I'm getting in the way of your little slave girlies. Or slave boys. Whatever you're currently into fucking—"

Her voice cut off in a gasp as he grabbed her hair from behind and yanked her head back. His cheek brushed hers, rough against her softness. "Stop right there." His voice was ice, a warning she couldn't ignore. "I'm telling you something, if you'd stop the childish jealousy and sniping long enough to hear my words. *I haven't been with anyone.* Did you hear it that time?" His fingers tightened in her hair. She clamped her lips shut, afraid to move or make a sound. "You had a past, and you changed. You changed for your Master. I would change for you, Molly. But not for this. Not for these lies and ugly petty jealousies. Not for this hollow person you've become."

He released her as abruptly as he'd grabbed her and stalked away. The solid wall at her back was gone, and she was left tottering on her feet. The door slammed with a clap of noise and Molly strained to hear a key turn in the lock. She wanted him to lock her in, to give at least that little sign that he still valued and cared for her, but cruelly, he left it open.

Like her Master, he knew exactly how to hurt her the most.

CHAPTER SIX
TIME

Mephisto lingered in the recessed sitting room of a dimly lit boutique as his friend Lorna helped a gay couple outfit their new slave in luxurious—and expensive—leather fetish wear. Lorna's Boutique had been serving the Seattle community for over a decade, catering to the serious pervert who was willing to pay for the best fetish gear available. It helped that Lorna herself was deliciously twisted. Gay or straight, dom or sub, Mistress Lorna knew how to play along with people's dynamics and have them even more riled up for one another when they left the shop than when they came in. It was probably the main reason her business was so good.

She'd asked Mephisto many times to become a business partner, but he preferred to remain her friend. Her staunch loyalty was too important to risk on the vagaries of business and work. He came to see Lorna when he was in the mood for fun, when he was in the mood to watch her play with customers, and times like now, when he was conflicted and confused.

At last the gay trio exited the store with their bags of clothes and toys, all three of them in heightened spirits. They'd be fucking like maniacs within the hour, Mephisto thought to himself. Lucky bastards.

Lorna chuckled as she sashayed her way back to him, her feminine hips and breasts the object of so much worship from those who submitted to her. She flicked at one of his dreadlocks and gave a teasing smile as she settled into the chair beside his. "She still has you in chastity, I see."

"What? Who?"

"Your little kitten. Clayton's old slave. She *is* the reason you haven't been partaking of your various fucktoys with your usual...how can I put it? Fervor? Gusto?"

Mephisto shrugged. "I've been busy, that's all."

Lorna's pale amber eyes narrowed and she snickered. "Lying too. You've got it bad for her."

Mephisto relaxed back in his chair and shot her a look. "Okay, what have you heard?"

"That she's been living in your spare room for months now. That she won't come out to play, not with you or anyone else. That you moon after her and fret about her, and that the two of you had a fight on Saturday night." She paused. "That you won't even sleep with Lila anymore."

He raised an eyebrow. "Lila told you that, I suppose."

"I've heard it from several people. Is it true?"

"Lila and I have been growing apart for some time."

Lorna waved a hand. "Forget Lila. What's going on with you and Molly? Forgive me for saying so, but you haven't been acting like yourself and everyone knows it. It's not like you to be..." Lorna's voice trailed off and she became very interested in her ostentatiously manicured nails.

"Not like me to be what?" he prompted.

"To be topped by a neurotic piece of slave meat. That's what."

Mephisto's hackles rose. "She's not slave meat. Her name is Molly."

Lorna laughed. "I know her name. Everyone does. But I notice you don't dispute the neurotic part. I've heard some stories about that girl that make me wonder."

He knew this was all part of Lorna's bluntness, her tough love, but it was still hard to keep his temper in check. "Molly is a smart woman, and she's really good at the lifestyle. She's just confused right now."

"She's confused, or you're confused?"

His dark eyes met Lorna's light ones. Contact lenses. He was one of few people who knew her eyes were really as dark as his own. And Lorna...Lorna knew his secrets too.

"Yes, I'm confused," he finally admitted. "I want her, and I think she wants me, but nothing...nothing is happening as easily as I expected it to." He sighed and rested his head on his hands. "Me and Clayton had this agreement that I would look after Molly if anything happened to him. And I thought... I guess I assumed she'd fall into my arms and we'd go on very much like she and Clayton did."

"But you're nothing like Clayton."

"I know."

"And you didn't take into consideration that she might have some feelings neither one of you could control."

Mephisto sighed, a great, shuddering, soul-baring sigh. "Yes. She is proving very difficult to control."

Lorna reached out for his hand and stroked it gently. "Ah, that's hard. It's so hard when they don't do what we want them to."

Mephisto laughed, her humor a balm for the turmoil in his brain. "It is hard. And I feel like I'm letting down Clayton."

"You're looking after her. She's at your place. She's not out there getting high and drunk and doing God knows what she used to do before Clayton pinned her down."

"But she's not happy. She's...she's fighting her nature. She says she doesn't want to be a slave anymore, that she doesn't want the lifestyle."

"Good God."

"I know. Now she's met this guy. They talk on the phone, they meet for lunch. He's taken her out to dinner a couple times. Vanilla ice cream for dessert, I'm sure." He shook his head and looked up into the eyes of his friend. "And she's convinced herself this is what she wants, but I know her. I know he won't make her happy."

75

"And you would?" Her incisive words flayed Mephisto's ego.

"I could try!"

"She's not polyamorous, my friend. Nor does she love casually. Don't you remember how she and Clayton were together?"

He stood and started pacing. "We could make it work. I could compromise. She could compromise."

"Relationships shouldn't be about compromise," Lorna argued. "They should be about people fulfilling one another."

"Fulfilling one another? Me and Molly are way past fulfillment." He paused, leaning against the wall. "Don't you get it? We're just meant to be. I burn so bad for her, Lorna. I always did, even when she was with Clayton. There was this pull between us even then, this excruciating pull, and it's still there now. When we're together it's like something's eating me up inside to possess her. She feels it too, I know. It's terrifying, so I don't blame her for wanting to run away from it. Before, there was Clayton to protect us from each other, but now..."

Lorna stared at Mephisto, a smile playing around her lips. "Are you telling me this girl has the power to drag you into a real relationship? Make you into a one-woman man?"

He collapsed back in the chair. "I don't know. Maybe. I feel like if I had her, I wouldn't want anyone else. I've dreamed of her service for so long. Dreamed of owning her, having her kneeling at my feet. If I had her, how could I want anyone else?"

"Have you told her this?"

"I've tried. Not in so many words, but..."

"Maybe you need to use more words."

God, more words. The words he'd used thus far seemed to mess things up more than they helped. "When we talk, the right words never come out. She's so afraid of me."

Lorna was silent a moment. "Maybe she has reason to be. Maybe she needs to come to terms with her fears before she comes into your arms. Maybe it's best that way."

Mephisto shook his head. "She's not even thinking about my arms. Only how to escape them. Every time this Eliot guy calls her I feel like

I'm losing her a little more. God, I've never felt so out of control in my life and I fucking hate it. It fucking sucks."

Lorna made a soft sound and stood to cross behind him. She rubbed his shoulders and leaned down to give him a squeeze. "I know how hard it is for people like you and me to lose control, how confused it can make you feel. I would offer to beat you into lucidity again but I have a feeling you'd refuse. Or finally manage to top me, which I'd never live down. Just remember, she's not doing this to hurt you. I really believe that. She needs time."

"How much time?" His voice sounded whiny, like a child. Maybe he did need a good beating from Lorna to get his head clear.

His friend looked up as a new customer walked in the door. She turned back to Mephisto. "Look, that's up to her. You have to give her all the time she needs. But think about this. If it's really so inevitable that you two come together...if you really burn for her as you say, and she feels the same about you, then it won't go away. At some point, you'll both have to give in to it. It's just a time game now. Be patient."

"Patient?" Mephisto made a very impatient sound. "Why can't we just force them to do everything we want? Coerce them into fulfilling our heart's desire?"

"Because, Master Mephisto, persuasion is a lot more interesting than coercion. A lot more legal too," she added as she went to attend the new customer. "Now go find something to do besides moping around my shop."

* * * * *

Molly stared down at the marble headstone, the velvety green grass. The neat row of flowers she'd planted a couple weeks before still thrived in the late summer sun, and the wind rustled the leaves in nearby trees, creating a peaceful, susurrating sound.

She didn't know why she'd wanted to bring Eliot here.

She supposed it was because they'd become so close. Acquaintance had become friendship, and friendship had steadily become something more. Courtship. He stood beside her now, quiet, but not freaked out. Eliot wasn't the kind of guy who got freaked out. He was the kind of guy who would take the hand of a girl he liked and squeeze it while they both looked down at her late husband's grave.

"He was lucky," Eliot said. "Lucky to be so loved. There are so many disastrous marriages out there. So many people hurting each other, so much cruelty. You guys must have had something special."

Without thought, Molly's fingers went to her neck, tracing the ghost of a metal collar. "We did."

"What was he like? I mean, was he funny? Serious? What did he like to do? Where did he work?"

Molly thought a moment. Where to begin to explain about her Master? Eliot obviously hadn't recognized his name or his position as a Seattle business magnate, not that she worried any more about Eliot being the avaricious type. She'd assured Mephisto that Eliot's sense of justice was too strong for him to take advantage of anyone, especially a new widow. Mephisto had grumbled that you never really knew anyone. Which was the truth.

"He, uh, worked in real estate," Molly said. "And he wasn't funny in a wacky way, no, but he had a great sense of humor. He was more the cultured, refined person, but kind. So kind."

"Cultured and refined?" Eliot laughed. "Nothing like me then."

"He was kind like you."

He squeezed her hand harder. Eliot was one of the kindest men she'd ever met aside from Clayton. Maybe this was all part of some big plan, this kind, new man catching her eye at Mack's Diner. If she was honest with herself, part of the reason she'd brought Eliot here was because she wanted Clayton to meet him in some cosmic way. Clayton would have approved of Eliot, she was sure of that. For all his silliness and flirtation, Eliot was a consummate gentleman. Even after two lunch meetings and four weeks of more serious dates, Eliot hadn't done anything but kiss her. It was like he waited for some sign from her that it was okay to move forward.

Molly was ready to move forward now.

She wanted more than kisses. She wanted...more. *I'll always love you, Master. But what do you think of this guy?*

There was no guidance, of course. She was on her own. She could ask Mephisto his opinion on Eliot, but that would involve the two of them meeting, and somehow Molly didn't want to mix those worlds. She still hadn't told Eliot where she lived, choosing to meet him instead "after work," at some convenient location near Mephisto's place. It was dishonest, but what choice did she have? What would Eliot think if he knew she lived in the back rooms of a fetish club? Before it got to that point, she'd move out, move back into Clayton's place.

But when she thought of leaving Mephisto's, she got a sick, nervous ache in her heart. Mephisto was still her safety net, her anchor. *I haven't been with anyone.*

"Well," Molly said. "Thanks for coming here. So what now? Do you want to walk around downtown?"

"Sure. We'll get some dinner and maybe... I don't know. Wanna go to a club? Dancing?"

"Maybe," Molly hedged. "Or maybe we could just go to your place and watch a movie. Or something."

Did that still work as a secret hook up code? It had been so long since Molly dated normally, since she engineered make out sessions and sleepovers. Would she sleep with Eliot? Was she ready? Hell, yes. She believed she was, and if the look on his face was any indication, he got her message loud and clear.

"Yeah, that sounds fun. I've got a thousand DVDs. Too many. I'm sure we could find something cool to watch. Curl up on the couch together and all that."

Oh, they were going to curl up all right. Molly felt a sudden urgent need for sex, for carnal, deep connection, and there was no fear. Just desire, and want. Safety in the arms of this wonderful, generous man. All through dinner she ached for him and craved his touch. She pictured him naked while they chatted over tapas and margaritas. By the time they got to his place, Molly was almost too wrought up to take in the surroundings, although they were very nice. Comfortable furniture, modern, organized layout. He would make a great lawyer, she decided. Detail oriented.

And yes, he had a huge DVD collection. Molly couldn't glean much from his library except that his tastes were eclectic and unpredictable. Choosing a film to watch was an exercise in negotiation. He wisely pushed romantic comedies, so Molly chose one she'd seen ages ago, a flick so iconic—and formulaic—she wouldn't really have to watch.

They sat on his couch, too full for popcorn, and sipped at glasses of wine. Molly took tiny swigs, letting the flavor sit on her tongue, and she waited. She didn't want to be too drunk when he finally made a move, and he seemed to feel the same way, because he didn't wait long. He started with light caresses in her hair. Oh God, the hair. He knew what he was doing. *Thank you, God.* She melted closer to him, laying a hand on his thigh. Casual, like she was just relaxing against him, but she felt his whole body tense in reaction, just for a moment. Then the deep breath.

They'd kissed before now, leisurely sweet kisses that reassured her and put her at ease. They kissed again like that, just for a bit, as he stroked and petted her hair, but then the kiss turned into something a little more serious. She tasted wine and passion, and the leashed sexuality that lurked beneath Eliot's polite exterior. *Yes, yes. Come out and play. I want it.*

He cupped her head in his hands, and his fingers tightened on her nape as he drew her closer. A small sigh of relief escaped. Relief that this was happening and it was really okay, and there was nothing wrong with her after all. She was just a normal girl with a hot, fun, wonderful guy making out on the couch while a stupid movie played in the background.

"Ah, you feel so good, Molly."

Eliot slid a hand down her arm, then across her chest to fondle one of her breasts. She leaned in to his touch, wanting something more insistent, but he was tentative. Polite. She gave a little moan of frustration. He must have interpreted it as encouragement because his arms tightened around her and then he was pushing her down, coming over her on the narrow sofa. He was a great kisser...exploring and responsive, and good about letting her come up for air before his lips latched over hers again. She had never been kissed by her Master like this. This was making out, and it was fun. They writhed against one another, chests and hips bumping, and then he pushed her leg to the side to settle between her thighs.

Molly arched, feeling the hard bulk of his cock between them, straining against his jeans. She reached for his waistband, popped the button. She whispered something. Maybe his name, maybe pleas for more, for him to touch her. She didn't know, only that she didn't want him to stop kissing her and pressing her down.

His hand came to her wrist. "Wait. Maybe we should move to the bedroom."

Molly made some equivocal noise, like "guh" or "unh," and let him help her up off the sofa. He took her hand and pulled her close and kissed her again, so gently, so sweetly, his fingertips beneath her chin. He walked her back toward his bedroom, staring over at her like he couldn't believe his luck. Ha. The way he kissed, she was his, full on.

His bedroom looked very much like the rest of his house. Organized, simply furnished, and comfortable. The bed had lots of pillows and a mod print comforter. Molly could imagine them lying there talking to one another, lazing away a Saturday afternoon or a Sunday morning. She turned to Eliot, waiting for him to take her, to sweep her off her feet, but all she got was a shy smile and more wonder-gazing.

"God, Molly." He reached out to cup her chin again. More kissing. Yeah, she liked the kissing...but she needed more. She pressed against him like a cat, wanting him to grab her, squeeze her. Overcome her.

"Come on," he said with a smile.

That was all she got. A nudge toward the bed, but no impassioned possession. They laid down side by side and kissed some more. He touched her skillfully, but skill wasn't enough to turn her on. Something was missing, some force or intensity. He slid her clothes off when she wanted him to rip them off, and then he set about doing everything he could to please her.

But she wanted to be the one to please him.

He trailed kisses down her waist, to her pelvis, and lower. She wanted to clamp her legs shut. She knew what was coming, knew he would go down on her and do everything he could to cater to her needs. That's what nice guys did. She laid back and tried to relax, tried to get into his lovey, gentle vibe, but nothing came, only frustration.

"You taste so sweet," he whispered against her mons. "You're so beautiful down here. You taste so fine, baby."

She made a soft sound, trying to play along, like he was arousing her. He was great at going down. He was spectacular at it, actually, if technique and enthusiasm were the markers. Any other girl would be coming like mad by now. She grasped his hair and tried to psych herself into pleasure. *Don't be stupid. This should feel good. The only reason it doesn't is because you're a sicko and you want him to tie you up and beat you instead.* Her soft sound became more of an impatient sigh.

Eliot stopped. "What's wrong?"

Molly squeezed her eyes shut and shook her head. "Nothing. I'm just... I've never been into this."

He laughed. "That's a new one. Well, what are you into?"

She caught the edge of annoyance in his voice. Shit. She was ruining everything. What was she supposed to do? Tell him everything she was into and watch him run for the hills? "Just fuck me," she said, pulling at his shoulders. "Please fuck me. I'm so hot for you."

The problem was, with every moment that passed, she grew a little less hot for him. She squeezed his shoulders, scratched him to try to urge him to more intensity, but he gave her a look like she was confusing him, or maybe freaking him out.

"I'm sorry," she whispered.

"Don't be sorry." More kissing. More gentle caresses. "I just want to make you feel good. You're so sweet, so hot."

He produced a condom, rolled it on and nestled the head of his cock against her pussy. He was hung nice and thick. She wanted him to thrust inside her roughly, thrust inside so it hurt a little and unsettled her. Instead he took his time, sinking into her in a sensual slide, lifting her hips to ease the way. Oh God, it felt good. It felt damn good to be filled again, but he was so tentative and gentle that any of the thrill of his entry dissipated into a kind of stupor of...ugh...sweetness.

"That feels good," she breathed. "You don't have to be so gentle. I want you."

"I know, baby. I want you too. It feels so good inside you."

He quickened his pace, but he was still as polite and vanilla as any lover could possibly be. He was exactly the lover she should have expected him to be: attentive, patient, caring. He was an excellent lover, an unselfish lover. The lover of any woman's dreams—but not hers.

He fucked her on and on, never tiring. He was waiting for her to come, but it wasn't happening. He caressed her, licked her nipples, kneaded her ass, but it was hopeless. None of it was right. When he flipped over on his back and pulled her on top of him, Molly gave up completely. It frightened her to be in this dominant position, and worse, he went still beneath her. "Ride me, babe. You're in charge now. Do what feels good."

"I can't. I...I never come in this position."

"I can make you come."

He moved in her a little, twisting his hips. Molly was going dry, so each thrust felt a little sharper, but it wasn't sexy pain. It was just pain. It was failure and misery. Even if she told Eliot what she was into, even if he got a little kinkier to fulfill her, that's just what it would be. To fulfill *her*. Ugh.

"Come for me, baby. I want to see you come."

It was clear Eliot was all about pleasing his partners, and that extended to getting them off. His face was screwed into a mask of concentration, like if he just tried hard enough he could make this happen.

It wasn't going to happen. He was still urging her on, making her buck up and down on his cock. She closed her eyes and tried to think about something to get turned on. Immediately her mind went to dark eyes and dreadlocks. Mephisto bending her over, forcing his cock into her ass and pounding his hips against her. No, it wasn't right for her to think about Mephisto, not in Eliot's bed. She looked down at him, focusing on him, on how much she wanted to come just to make him happy. Nothing. Nothing at all. "It's starting to hurt a little," she said.

He rolled with her again. She barely suppressed a sigh as he spread her legs, trying to work her clit, trying to coax some response that wasn't there. Molly wanted to disappear, to bolt from his place and hide somewhere and cry and scream and rage. He kissed her breasts, then slid his tongue around the base of her neck. She thought about her Master's collar that used to rest there...

"I don't have any lube," he said. "Maybe if I put on a new condom—"

"No," Molly said. Enough. No more. She forced a smile and touched his arm. "It's okay. Sometimes I just don't come."

"I could go down on you again."

"No."

Eliot deflated a little, rolled back and away from her. "I'm sorry. I'm sorry it's not working for you."

"You can still come," Molly offered. "You can fuck me until you come. Or I could go down on you."

He shook his head, looking a little horrified. "No, I wouldn't expect that from you." His previously impressive hard-on was faltering before her eyes, fading away in the face of his self-perceived failure as lover. Molly steeled herself against tears and tried to sound casual.

"You know, it's not you. It's me. You're a wonderful lover. You're really skilled in bed. I mean it, you are."

He gave her a rueful smile. "Circumstances would seem otherwise."

She knew if she explained the problem to him, that she needed him to be more forceful, more dominant, that he'd take a stab at it just to make her happy, but he would never be like her Master. Never be like Mephisto, a man for whom control and domination came as naturally as breathing. But Eliot was such a great guy... Maybe in time, she could learn to get aroused by gentleness and equality between the sheets.

Or maybe it was time to face the fact that she was wired weird and always would be.

Tears filled her eyes and this time she couldn't hold them back. "I'm sorry."

"No, I'm sorry," Eliot crooned, stroking her cheek. "I'm sorry we didn't wait longer. I think maybe we tried this too soon."

Molly shook her head. "No. I think I just...I miss my husband. I still miss him too much. You're so different from him."

Eliot's face softened. While it wasn't the exact truth, it was enough to make him feel a little less of a failure, and she was glad of that. He tried to pull her close again, but she scooted away, stood to get her clothes. "I think... I think I have to leave for now. I'm sorry."

I'm sorry I can't stop crying. I'm sorry I can't find myself and you got caught up in all my craziness.

"You don't have to go," he said. "We can finish watching the movie. I can hold you. Molly, you're upset."

She swiped away the tears that threatened to drown her. "I'll be fine."

He began to dress too, seeming to find his own solace in looking after her. "Let me hold you until you stop crying anyway."

"I don't want you to hold me!" Her sudden sharp outburst surprised even her. "I don't want you to comfort me, or fix me. I want to be left alone right now. You're not the right person for me, okay?"

He put his hands up in a defensive motion. "Okay. Fine. Blunt, slightly rude. But okay. Can I call you a cab?"

"No, I'll walk."

It was far to walk, but he didn't argue or try to stop her. He did follow her all the way back to Mephisto's, along six city blocks in oppressive darkness, a silent specter lingering back and letting her have her little meltdown. Somehow it upset her even more, than he was still so kind when she'd basically dumped his ass. He deserved someone suitable for him, someone who would appreciate the chivalrous knight he was. Every time she thought about what might have been, about what she was passing up, tears blurred her eyes again and spilled onto her cheeks.

When she reached Club Mephisto, there were a few groups of kinky people smoking outside in their corsets and fetish gear. They called out to her, alarmed by her tears. She looked over her shoulder one last time at the man who'd been so much to her. Her first friend in a long time. She should have let him stay a friend. Now, with her meltdown and her late night flight to the doors of Seattle's best-known fetish club, she was afraid he'd have nothing more to do with her. She felt rage and deep depression. She wished she could see his smile one last time, but no. That would be the last straw, the last tragedy she could take. If he smiled at her now, it would destroy her.

Fortunately, he didn't. He only turned and walked back the way he'd come.

CHAPTER SEVEN
TEARS

The club was full of people, full of active noisy scenes when Molly returned from her date with her friend. Idiot. Eliot. Whatever his name was. Mephisto always waited for her while she was away, felt unsettled until she was back again. It was just after midnight when Molly came in, the witching hour. His gaze found her like a magnet seeking north, and riveted on her hollow expression, her red rimmed eyes.

She tried to creep off to her room without being seen, but Mephisto wasn't having it. He cut her off by the bar, tilting her head up although she struggled to keep it trained on the floor.

"I'll kill him," he said. "What did he do to you?"

"Nothing." She tried to push him away, but he stood firm.

"What did he do to you? Why are you crying?"

"It's over, okay?" She yelled at him over the club's low, pulsing music. "You should be happy."

Yes, Mephisto was happy—ecstatic—but he hated Idiot for making Molly cry. Not just cry, but bawl. She stumbled past him, muttering warnings for him to stay away. "Tell me what went down," he said, dogging her steps into the back rooms. "He didn't hurt you, did he?"

"Don't you have somewhere to be?"

"Answer my question."

She spun on him in the hallway. "No, he didn't hurt me. He just made me realize something I've been trying to deny about myself. That I'm not a nice girl. I'm not a *normal* girl." Her face twisted as she dissolved into more tears. "There's something really wrong with me, and it's never going to be fixed."

Mephisto took her arms, his body tensing in fury as he pressed her back against the wall. "God damn you, how many times do I have to tell you that nothing's wrong with you? How many times, girl, before you believe it?"

The "girl" reverberated between them like an alarm bell. Instead of letting her go, he pressed closer, trapping her with his chest, his arms. Her tears both disturbed and aroused him. He wanted to taste them. He lowered his head beside hers, brushed his jaw across her cheek, feeling the hot liquid like a burn. *I burn. I burn for you.* She shivered and shrank away from him.

"No. I don't want you."

Even as she said the words, she cried harder, her fingers curling and uncurling in the sleeves of his black tee. He felt the tips of her breasts slide like a tease across his chest. "I know, Molly. I know you don't want me. But you need me."

"No..."

"Nothing's wrong with you. I know who you are. I know what you need, baby."

She squeezed his shoulders now, ran her hands up into his dreadlocks with an intensity and violence he welcomed. He knew what she needed—what Eliot obviously hadn't been able to give her. He took her hands, pulled them down from his hair and slammed them against the wall on either side of her head. Her sobs cut off, replaced with a stuttering breath and a soft whine. Her lips parted as she blinked up at him.

He held her wrists even tighter as he kissed her. It wasn't a tender kiss. It was punishment for making him ache so bad, and a warning that she had about thirty seconds to save herself. To protest, to kick him in the nuts, to run off. Twenty seconds. Ten. He kissed her so hard they were both breathless. He could feel her pulse in his hands, or maybe it was his own rampaging heartbeat.

"Nothing's wrong with you that can't be fixed," he growled when they finally broke apart.

He grabbed a handful of her hair. His other hand slid to her ass and squeezed hard, pressing her forward against his throbbing erection. He kissed her again, long and deep, and then he shoved her to her knees right there in the hallway. She sank down without resisting. He ripped open his fly and yanked down his jeans, releasing his painfully engorged cock and nudging it into her mouth. He gave her a moment to find balance, to collect herself, and then he surged forward, forcing her head against the wall. Her sultry moan vibrated his shaft and balls.

Her hands came around his thighs, grasping, pulling him closer. "Yes, good girl," he crooned as he thrust into her face. "Good, good girl. Nothing wrong, is there? You just needed to be put in your place."

She murmured something around his cock. He pulled back. "What's that?"

"Yes, Master."

Pleasure, hot as fire, arced through him like lightning. "Say it again. 'Yes, Master. Thank you for putting me in my place.'"

"Yes, Master, thank you for putting me in my place."

He groaned and pulled her up by her hair. Not brutally. She was like liquid now, this beautiful slave, sliding along his jagged edges and settling into place. They were suddenly dancing, him and her, a choreography of dominance and submission that had always come to them with unexplained ease. He dragged her back to the bedroom, pushed her onto the bed and shoved her head down into the blankets. Her hands made fists beside her head as he slapped both her ass cheeks. Without thought, without pause, he drove inside her deep, fucking her hard. He slapped her thighs again, once, twice, feeling her tense around him from the pain. His hands ran up her sides, then forward to squeeze and cup the heaviness of her breasts. He pinched her nipples viciously between his fingernails only to hear her frantic cries.

She bucked back against him every bit as hard as he fucked her, searching for a release she'd doubtless needed for some time. He urged her on. "It's okay. Let go. Be my horny little slut. My whore. I love you this way."

Her hips twisted at his crass intimacies. She started making noises, and he felt them as intensely as he felt each stroke into her tight, hot sheath. His legs shook, his balls drew up in excruciating tension. Her hands clenched on his bed sheets and her legs opened farther. She threw her head back and wailed as she contracted around him.

He grabbed her waist and drilled her, his own orgasm seconds away. Until the end, he intended to pull out, to splash his cum over her as a claiming, a mark of dominance, but at the last minute he stayed buried inside her. It didn't matter. He knew she couldn't get pregnant. They were both recently tested and clean. He wanted to stay inside her, to fill her with his release, and so he did, jerking with the novelty of emptying himself in her hot, welcoming depths. By slow degrees, his fingers relaxed their hold on her hips, leaving red marks behind.

"Okay," he whispered, running a hand up her back to soothe her trembling. "Okay. You're okay now."

Okay. Yes. This had been inevitable all along. Mephisto pushed her down on the bed, flipped her over. She was wide-eyed, perhaps expecting more violence, more demand. Not that she wouldn't enjoy those things, but he didn't feel like giving them to her just now. Instead he gave her tenderness and warmth. He slid one knee between her legs, gathering her close and cradling her. He brushed her hair back from her face and dropped kisses on her cheeks, her chin. He nuzzled her ear and marveled at the calm that settled over him. He wasn't sure if this was the start of something more, something serious, or just a much-needed release for both of them, but either way, he was grateful for it. Holding her was a balm. Delicious relief.

"Ah, Molly," he whispered against her ear. "I've missed you so much."

He could feel her smile against his cheek. "I've been right here."

"You haven't been here in a while. Not the Molly I remembered." Mephisto leaned back after a moment, touching a lock of her hair, and then brushed her eyelids with his lips. "What did Eliot do to you? He didn't humiliate you, did he? Mock you?"

"No." Molly toyed with the end of one of his dreadlocks, then traced a meandering Celtic tattoo up and over his shoulder. "I didn't even tell him about me. About my past, my slavery. All he did was have sex with me. He was very generous, very sweet."

"Ah." Mephisto nodded. "Too sweet?"

"I thought it would be fine. That being with a normal, vanilla guy would feel just as good as being with a lifestyle guy, only different. I really liked him a lot, and I was excited about being with him, you know, intimately. But it was awful. It actually upset me. It's hard to explain."

"You don't have to explain. I've been there. I've tried to tone myself down to be with vanilla women because I was physically attracted to them, mentally attracted to them, whatever." He laughed. "It never works. Not only does it not work. It's—"

"Wretched," Molly supplied, laughing too. "Awkward. Excruciating. Weird."

"All of the above." He looked down at the woman in his arms. Her laughter seemed a miracle to him, after so many tears and so much frustration. If Eliot was the one who brought her to this place, he couldn't hate the man, not completely. "So what did you tell him? Did you just leave?"

"Sort of. I guess I'll have to talk to him like an adult at some point, give him more of an explanation."

"You should. It would be the polite thing to do, if he was as kind and friendly as you say."

She shifted, brushing her hair back from her face, and let out a frustrated sigh. "I wish me and him could stay friends. I know we can't, but still. That's the saddest thing of all. Losing his friendship."

Mephisto knew this was the point when he should tell her that maybe she could stay friends with Eliot. That maybe love could transcend things like sexuality and history if given enough time. But part of him knew that would only lead to more heartbreak down the line, and it had been difficult enough to see her tears before. "I'm sorry, Molly. You must feel terribly disappointed and sad at the moment. Please understand that what just happened between us wasn't some attempt to take advantage of you. It was just..." He pulled her closer, breathing in her smell, basking in her warmth. "It just felt right to do at the time. Are you okay? Do you want to leave and go to your room, or do you want to sleep here?"

"What do you want?"

He would have to start giving her less choices. If she was going to transition into his slave, they had to find a starting point. "Here's what I want. While I'm helping close down Club Mephisto, I want you to go and shower, brush your teeth, and get back into my bed wearing nothing at all. You don't have to stay up for me if you're too sleepy, but I can't promise I won't wake you when I return. If you're in my bed, it's going to be hard to keep my hands off you."

She gave him a surrendered, sweet smile that reminded him so much of Clayton's old Molly he almost gawked. Almost fell on her again, consuming her submission like some long denied delicacy. No...the club. He had to help with the club. Later. Later, more Molly, more submission, more of that lovely smile.

When he returned, she was sleeping like an angel. Mephisto slid into his bed beside her, breathing in her fragrant wet hair, the light floral scent of her skin. Beneath it all, some wild, seductive undercurrent connected him to her, as natural as sunshine, as constant as the blood in his veins. For the first time in a long time, he slept in peace.

* * * * *

Molly woke to his words. "I want you." His deep voice rumbled in her ear and resonated down between her legs. She was manipulated and moved, turned onto her back. She sleepily complied. He slid over top of her, pinching one nipple, drawing her from restfulness to alert attention.

She became aware of a rock hard cock poking against her thigh, and heated arousal bloomed between her legs in response.

She looked into his eyes, into those depths that were so familiar and yet always such a fearsome mystery to her. He caressed her, preparing her for his onslaught. His hands communicated will and intention. Last night, Molly had called him Master. The word had come so easily, without prompting, and this was why. "I want you too. Please."

He was power and threat but he was softness too, and solid reassurance on this morning when things were changing for Molly again. Mephisto shifted so his cock nudged hot and insistent between her pussy lips. "I didn't use protection last night. But I'm clean. I assume you still are too."

Molly turned the words over in her lust-addled brain, remembered that she couldn't get pregnant, and yes, if they were both clean... Was he asking her for permission? Were they fluid bonding now? Things were moving so fast, but she had no desire to slow them down. She lifted her hips to meet his, which he took for the capitulation it was. As he reached down between them to stroke her clit and finger her wetness, she felt a combination of confusion and horniness. He was being slow, gentle, just like Eliot, but it was like night and day between them. What was the difference? How could it feel icky when Eliot was gentle with her, but fire-sexy-hot when Mephisto was gentle?

Because Mephisto was only gentle every once in a while. Mephisto rationed gentle so that when he used it, it felt a hundred times more gentle than gentleness from anyone else. It was a violent kind of gentle that most guys could never replicate.

How kind Mephisto was, to give her this sweetness just when she needed it, when she doubted and wondered and was searching in her heart for the answer to questions, the greatest one being *What do I want?* Right now, she wanted Mephisto. That was simple, uncomplicated truth, and there was no force or scening to distract her from it now. She just wanted him, his touch, his attention—and oh, how erotic it felt when he moved into her skin-to-skin, no condom dampening the intimacy. He felt so strong and encompassing hovering over her. His thick tool spread her pussy wide and he surged forward, forward, forward until there was nowhere else to go. She clung to him, reeling from the fullness. He paused until she moved her hips, and then they were both in motion, thrusting, fucking, groping to get closer.

He gasped her name, but she wasn't sure what she said back to him. Pleas and whispers that made no sense, except that they urged him on. Each stroke was hot, demanding, a brazen slide in and out, but his hands were soft. His voice was a whisper at her ear. There was no time, no thought, just this sweet joining, and for Molly, a shuddering climb to a climax that threatened to destroy her. She hadn't felt joy or closeness like this since she'd been with her Master. It felt so very much like...love.

"Mephisto!" She grasped at him, her arms around his neck. He kissed her as her moans rose in intensity, smothering her gasp of culmination. Her whole pelvis contracted into squeezing, glorious waves. He grunted and bucked inside her, driving her across the bed. He leaned on one elbow, his dreadlocks tickling her face as he gave one final snap of his hips and emitted a long, low growl, followed by a guttural "Jesus!" They both came to rest, gasping for breath.

Love, love...love. You love him, Molly.

Out of the frying pan and into the fire. She couldn't love Mephisto. He didn't have room in his life for love, not the kind of love she wanted. Eliot had had room, but they hadn't been sexually compatible. What kind of joke was her life turning into? She chanced a look up at Mephisto only to find him frowning down at her in that scary, penetrating way he had.

She gazed back at him, swallowing hard. "So...um. Am I your slave now?"

Mephisto blinked. "Why would you ask me that?"

"I don't know. You said we could exchange power non-sexually. But now we...we had sex. Twice."

Mephisto sighed and smiled a little. "You don't go straight from friendship to slavery, even if you've had amazing sex. Twice. Did you immediately become Clayton's slave? You dated first, didn't you? You got to know one another."

"But you and I have known each other for years."

"Yes. As friends." He cupped her face and kissed her nose, her eyes. "Anyway, you don't have to look so alarmed. If you don't want to be my slave, you don't have to be."

As if she could lie there in his arms and not want to be enslaved to him. That was the problem. Everyone wanted to be Mephisto's slave, but he'd never had a serious relationship she knew of. "I think I'm alarmed because I do want to be your slave," she admitted. "But I don't know how it would work out."

She looked away, struggling against a maelstrom of emotion, but Mephisto forced her gaze back to his. "One step at a time," he said. "Let's try being lovers. I want to be your lover. I think you want to be my lover. From that, let's see where it goes. Let's not barrel headlong into slavery. I know you were deep into slavehood at one time, but then, remember? You decided it wasn't for you. I think we should take it slowly this time, okay?"

Yes, Sir. Yes, Master. His voice always made everything clear, always made everything seem squared away. He was still pressed against her, his cock somehow still hard between her legs. He moved a little, the lines of his face relaxing into a tender, almost shy grin.

"This reminds me of that morning," he said. "The last morning you were with me. Do you remember?"

She ducked her head into his shoulder. "How on earth could I not remember?"

He stroked her all over. Her shoulders, her back. Her breasts and stomach, her arching hips. Like that morning long ago, they fell back into pleasure, taking no note of time. He touched her in any way he could make her react, and praised her every time she came. She knew he could just as easily refuse to let her come, torment her for his pleasure, lock her into chastity for days or even weeks. If she became his, she'd have to put up with that and anything else that moved his sadistic side. But for now, making her come was moving him, and she was determined to enjoy every moment of it. He said she should take it slowly, and she would.

Because Mephisto wouldn't give her any other choice.

CHAPTER EIGHT
LOVE

Eliot didn't take her calls. He didn't come looking for her, even though he'd walked her home and knew where to find her. So for three Fridays, Molly waited at Mack's Diner. Now it was the fourth Friday again. She sat very straight at her table in the corner, with her book and her sandwich and sometimes a slice of apple pie. She was off the cherry. It made her sad now. If he stayed away much longer, she'd have to turn to lemon meringue.

In her book was an envelope she had to deliver to him, but he was making it hard. She could have dropped it off at the UPS Center nearby, but she wasn't sure a note she left there would find its way to him. And this was a really important note.

Dear Eliot, she'd written.

I'm so sorry for running out on you that night. I panicked, for reasons too complicated to explain here. I'm sorry we didn't work out, but I don't regret our friendship. You helped me in ways I could never explain. I'll just say I'm very thankful. On that note, I hope you will accept this token of my appreciation.

Ugh, "token of my appreciation." It sounded so cheesy and impersonal, but she'd never been much of a writer. It was almost noon and the diner was filling up. Around 12:10 she felt deep disappointment. He wasn't coming. Maybe he'd never come back. Maybe he would avoid Mack's Diner like the plague forevermore because of her. Then at 12:15, he and a group of his buddies showed up.

When she saw him there, right there, as handsome and smiling as ever, she couldn't help but admire him. She also wanted to disappear. What would he do when he saw her? What would he say? Maybe he would ignore her, pretend he didn't see her. But no. His eyes scanned the diner and latched onto hers almost immediately. His smile faded and Molly felt a sinking in her stomach. He headed toward her with a grim look on his face. He slid into the chair at her table, his back to his friends, and gave her a look that was pretty antagonistic.

"Hi, Molly."

"Hi, Eliot." They both breathed in and out and the waitress materialized at that exact awkward moment to take his order. Eliot asked for a turkey club. After the waitress left he looked back at her, tapping his fingers on the table. Molly stared at those fingers. He had nice, clean, well-manicured hands for a delivery guy. She said, "I tried to call you a few times."

"I've been busy." Eliot shook his head and rubbed his neck. "No. I haven't been busy. I just don't think... You and I..."

She put a hand over his. "You don't have to say it. I know."

He pursed his lips and Molly remembered what a wonderful kisser he was. She played with the edges of the envelope tucked into her book.

"Listen, Eliot, I wasn't completely honest with you about who I am or...well...a lot of things. Not for any insidious purpose. Just because my life has been a mess lately. That wasn't a lie."

He looked at her for a long moment. "Are you really a new widow? Or was all that made up?"

"No, that wasn't made up. I'm just..." She squeezed her forehead with both hands, then gazed up at him, searching for words to explain. "I guess the two main things I didn't tell you—that I should have—are that I'm very rich and I'm very weird."

Nothing she was saying was cracking his cool facade. "Rich and weird, huh?"

The waitress was back, dropping a sandwich and cola in front of him on her way to another table. Molly waited as he started eating, took a sip of her own drink for calm.

"So how rich? And how weird? What do you mean by weird?" Before she could answer, he burst out in sharp, defensive words that made her feel sad. "You know, it's my fault. I should have known you weren't— I mean, I could see something was going on with you, but I don't know." He shrugged and swallowed hard. "I liked you."

"I liked you too. We were good friends. And none of this is your fault. It's my fault."

"*It's my fault.' 'It's your fault.'* This is a stupid conversation. At the end of it, things just didn't work out with us. It's cool."

Molly grimaced. "Is it cool? You don't seem cool."

"Well, I'm not cool." He put his sandwich down and leaned closer to her. "I have this awful feeling of incompletion, like the things I wanted to happen between us didn't come true. I'm disappointed."

"I know," Molly said quickly. "I feel that too."

"But at the same time, you made it pretty clear I'm not 'the right person' for you."

"I'm sorry."

"Don't be sorry. I appreciate your honesty. But I can't be glad. I can't be all like, 'oh, hi, Molly, great to see you' and shoot the shit like we're just friends now."

"I would never ask that of you."

He made a soft, reproachful noise. "Then why are you here?"

She reached into her book and slid the envelope from the pages, pushed it across the table to him. "I wanted to be sure you got this. I've thought about this a lot, and...well. Please open it."

After a moment of hesitation, he picked it up and pushed a finger along the envelope's flap. He unfolded her letter, straightened it, scanned it quickly. Then he opened the folded-up check that had fallen down onto the table beside his plate. He blinked at it for a few seconds.

"Uh." He narrowed his eyes and looked again. "This is a check made out for $300,000."

"It's for law school. So you don't have to work anymore while you get your degree."

"Molly..." Eliot frowned, then gave a small hysterical chuckle. "This is a check for *three hundred thousand dollars*."

"If you need more, let me know. But my late husband's lawyers said that should be plenty, even for a really good law school."

He shook his head and put a hand over his mouth. She knew what he was thinking. That it was too much, that she was giving it to him for the wrong reasons.

"Please take it," she said. "It's not a pay off, or because I feel guilty or bad. It's not anything, just me wanting to help you. Just me wanting to do something really generous for a deserving person. My husband would have liked his money going to someone like you. Someone who wants to make a difference."

He gave her an arch look. "How do you know I want to make a difference?"

"You wouldn't be working so hard to go back to school otherwise." She twisted her hands together. It's not like she'd expected him to jump up and down and hug her, but she'd hoped he might be happy, excited at least. "I have so much money I don't need. Please allow me to do this for you."

He looked down at the oblong, beige slip of paper in his hand and shook his head again. "I can't really believe this. Is this a joke?"

"I know you probably think I'm loony, but no. If you don't have a good place to put that much money, I have a lot of financial advisors who'd be happy to help you set something up."

There was an edge of anger in his piercing gaze. "A lot of financial advisors? An army of them, huh? When would you have told me how rich you are? That you can cut your friends three-hundred-thousand-dollar checks just because you want to help?"

"I didn't think it was important. I didn't think you'd care."

Eliot put the check down in front of him, smoothed it out, scrubbed his hands down his cheeks, and then picked it up again. "What the fuck, Molly."

It was a statement, not a question, so she didn't reply, just sat and waited. He would take the money or he wouldn't. She wanted him to have it, even if he was acting like an ass, but if he refused it she would live with that too.

"I just don't understand why you're doing this," he finally said, his face still obscured with one hand.

Molly searched for the right words to say, to make him okay with it. "You know, I have a lot of lawyers, but they're old. My husband's old lawyers. Maybe I'll need a younger lawyer one day. A really kind, young lawyer with a lot of integrity and an actual sense of humor."

His face twisted. "You always say I'm kind. It sounds so...blech. It's like saying someone's *nice*."

Molly flushed. She'd probably described him as "nice" to Mephisto and her husband's lawyers about a hundred times by now. "Whatever. Do you see what I'm saying? I'm going to need people on my side, people I can trust, people I know. It would be great if one of them was you."

"So this money comes with an entail, is that it? I can have it as long as I work for you when I have my JD."

"Work for me?" Molly threw up her hands. "I don't own a law firm. But once you're out there lawyering or whatever, you can be hired? Right?"

"If I get into the kind of law you'll need. Which sounds like financial law. Business."

"Real estate, mostly."

"I was thinking more about criminal law. Courtroom stuff. I don't know. I guess I'm not really sure where law school will lead me."

"You won't become one of those horrible personal injury lawyers, will you? With those fake, sensationalist ads, offering people a free consultation?"

"Free consultations?" He seemed to consider that. "I don't know. My time will be valuable. Maybe free toasters."

Molly wrinkled her nose and they both laughed. Eliot ran a hand down the front of his work shirt, his expression thoughtful and finally a bit more relaxed. "All right. Wow. This is really a life changer for me. No more brown uniform." He laughed abruptly, gave her his biggest, brightest smile. "I'm a stuttering moron over this. I'm sorry. Molly, thank you. I don't deserve this, I don't know how to repay you for it, but God, I'm so thankful for this. I'm sorry if I'm acting stupid." He shook his head with a kind of wonder. "It's just a really big surprise."

"But it's a really big *pleasant* surprise, isn't it?"

"Pleasant? That might not be a strong enough word." He waggled his eyebrows at her. "My sugar mama has finally arrived."

Molly sobered and looked down at the cover of her book. "I won't demand any young lovin' in return. Not that I didn't—" God, why did she bring that up? "I feel like I have to explain—"

"I wish you wouldn't."

"No, I have to."

"No." He took a deep breath. "I know what Club Mephisto is. That place I followed you to. I asked around. You own it?"

Molly felt a wild urge to laugh at that idea, but the moment wasn't that funny. "I don't own it. I'm in a relationship with the owner."

"A *relationship*." She could see the veiled distaste, hear the disapproval in his tone. "It's an S&M place, right? So I guess you're his, what, slave or whatever?"

"That's kind of private."

"But that's what they do there, isn't it? He beats on you? Chains you to the wall? That kind of thing?"

"Uh, not exactly." Of course Eliot wouldn't know. Of course he'd have misconceptions. She understood it, but it still annoyed her.

"How long have you known this guy?" Eliot's voice sounded tight. "He's a guy, I assume? The owner?"

"I've known him almost ten years."

That seemed to take a bit of the bluster out of him. "He knows you're giving me this money?"

"It's not his money. But yes, he knows. He encouraged me to."

"Is he in charge of your money? Don't give him control of your money, Molly."

Her lips curved slightly at the urgency in his tone. Eliot was determined to be kind and protective, even now. "Don't give him my money? Is that the advice of counsel?"

"Yes."

"Don't worry. My husband pretty much fixed it so no one can get at the money but me."

"Was your husband... Did he know you and this club owner...?"

"Mephisto. His name is Mephisto. Yes, my husband knew him well. Mephisto introduced us."

"Oh."

Molly stabbed at her untouched piece of pie. "It's complicated. It would be hard to explain the whole story."

"You don't have to. But if you were with him, why did you date me?"

"I wasn't with him when I met you." She screwed her eyes shut. "No, that's a lie. He was always there, but I wanted to be sure he was what I wanted. Or maybe...I hoped you would prove to me that I didn't want to be with him."

Eliot looked as puzzled as she felt when it came to Mephisto. "If you don't want to be with him, why are you with him now?"

"Because I have to be." Eliot's face went hard at that answer. Molly backtracked, holding up a hand. "No. Okay. A better way to say it is that I have to be with him because he's one of the few people who gets me."

"If you gave me more time, maybe I could have gotten you too," he said with a touch of reproach.

"Oh, Eliot. I don't know how to explain it. It's like... you meet a lot of people in life but there are people you meet who don't just become friends or lovers. They become this deeper, more mysterious thing.

There's something about them you can't forget, can't let go of. This almost painful connection. That's how it is with him and me."

Eliot traced over the edge of the check she'd given him, over her scrawled note. "I thought we had a connection like that. I don't know if I'll ever be able to forget you."

"You will. You'll be studying. Meeting smart, well-adjusted law school girls."

He made a face. "Is that what a 'nice' guy like me ends up with? A well-adjusted girl?"

Molly cut her eyes at him. "If you're lucky. Crazy sugar mamas like me are overrated. Be glad you'll never have to learn that firsthand."

Eliot looked at his watch, then back at her. It was time for him to go, time for this strange, affecting interlude to be over.

"I'm so glad I met you," she said. "I won't forget you. And I wish you all the best."

Eliot reached across the table and clasped her hand in a warm grip. "If you ever need anything... If that man doesn't treat you right..."

Molly shook her head. "He's a good person. Don't worry."

"His name is Mephisto," he pointed out. "He's named after the devil incarnate. The Dark Lord."

"Ha," said Molly. "His real name is Jay. Or Jason. Something like that. Wait. I think it's Jayden."

"You've known him for ten years and you don't know his real name?" Eliot shook his head. "You *will* need a good lawyer someday. I have a mission now. I'm going to work real hard to hone my skills."

It felt right to end with mirth and teasing. Someday some lucky woman would fall in love with Eliot, and Molly wouldn't begrudge her his sweetness, his smile. Molly needed a different kind of sweetness, a fact she'd finally come to terms with.

She would miss Eliot, but she understood now they were never meant to be.

* * * * *

Ah. God. Where was she?

Stupidly, Mephisto had warned Molly to take things slow, never considering how difficult it would be for him to follow his own advice.

Not that they weren't growing closer, finding intimacy. He played with her every day, after breakfast, or when she got home from her volunteer jobs or the violin lessons she'd begun again. He tied her up, toyed with her, gave her cage time and then took her out and fucked her into a puddle. But that was all it was between them for now, playing. Carefully choreographed scenes for feeling out boundaries and becoming familiar again. He was going slow for her, to make the transition smoother and kinder. She was fun to play with, to control, not that he ever did anything malicious to her. No, everything he did—even the cruelest things—came from his heart, the heart she'd taken over, moved into, and claimed as her own.

All he could think about was pulling her deeper and deeper into submission to him.

He wasn't going to force her into anything more encompassing, though, until she was ready. He was determined not to give her any ammunition to throw in his face later. He was giving her the time and space she needed, and he didn't mind because he knew she was steadily working her way to him. She was squaring things away with lawyers, with family. She was reading and sitting for long hours thinking and writing in a journal.

She was getting her ducks in a row. They both were. Mephisto had released his other play-slaves, and told his casual partners that he was experimenting with monogamy for now. That wasn't to say he'd never share Molly once she was his, or bring other partners into their dynamic, but now, at the beginning of what might be forever, they both had to be unfettered and available to one another one hundred percent.

Unfortunately that involved Mephisto staying back and letting Molly work out her relationships too, like smoothing the rough edges she'd left with Eliot. Every Friday she set out to find him, and Mephisto had to force himself to let her go. He'd busy himself with club work, invoices, promotion. Today he was party planning, sending emails and making calls about a shibari-themed play night coming up in a couple months. It wasn't like the vanilla guy was going to win her back somehow. Mephisto told himself that—repeatedly—but there was still the worry she wouldn't return to him. That she'd call Mephisto and say, "I made a mistake. We're compatible after all. Can you send over my stuff?"

From what Mephisto knew, Eliot was a stand up guy, which was the worst part of all of it. If Molly wanted him, Mephisto would have to usher her into the man's arms and smile the whole time he was doing it. Jesus Christ, it would suck.

"Mephisto."

He was startled out of his fretful thoughts by her voice. He looked up to find her walking through the play space toward him. He searched her expression and found some new softness there, some relief. She'd seen Eliot...and she'd come back to him. He held out his hand and pulled her close when she came near. He settled her in his lap and tilted her head back, threading his fingers in her soft dark hair. "Little Molly," he breathed against her lips.

He squeezed her breasts as she huddled against him, worked a hand down her front to grope her pussy through her jeans. When she was his, really his, her clothes would come off when they were alone together, when they were at home. He didn't like them coming between him and Molly's hot, wet pussy, her hard, thrusting nipples. He pushed her up off his lap with a grunt.

"Undress."

He stood at the same time to take off his shirt and kick off his jeans. "Did you see him?"

Molly stopped mid-strip. "Undress," he said again, sharply. "Talk to me at the same time. Did you see him?"

"Yes, Sir."

"How did it go?"

"It was..." She moaned softly as he sat back down and pulled her astride his lap. "Eliot was a little..."

"Surprised?"

"He seemed a little angry at first—oh!" Mephisto dug his fingers into her thighs and yanked her down hard on his cock, feeling her responsiveness, her reactions like a drug. Her pussy was so tight, a perfect glove.

"Angry? Angry how?" He jerked his cock in her so her tits bounced in front of him. It was impossible not to bite and suck them, and each vicious nibble resulted in a delicious clench of her pussy. He tightened his hands around her waist. "Didn't you give the guy three hundred thousand bucks?"

"Yes, Sir."

"So why...on...earth...would he be angry?" Mephisto punctuated each word with another deep thrust. Molly shook her head.

"I don't know. I think... Maybe..."

Mephisto precluded any further attempt at an answer with a commanding kiss. He broke away, pulling her head back to nuzzle and suckle her neck. He held her chin hard and licked her pale cheek, wanting to eat her alive, as always. She was too much, and simultaneously never enough. "Maybe he was angry that he's not going to be able to fuck your delicious pussy the way I am."

"Ohhh..." She shuddered. "Yes, Sir. That's probably it."

"He won't ever have your ass or your mouth either. I think that would make me feel angry too. He won't ever get to use any of your holes, will he?"

"No... No, Sir."

"Because you belong to me, Molly."

Molly, Molly, Molly... He used her name all the time, and he'd use it forever. Clayton hadn't used it much after he'd collared her. He'd called her "girl," in great part because Molly liked that type of objectification, but Mephisto preferred to keep her attached to her name. Attached to herself. He wanted all of her, not just the slave and the service. He wanted her mind, her intellect, her sensuality that exploded even now in his arms. He could always save "girl" for when she was in trouble. That would be fun.

"Are you going to come for me, you little slut?" Oh yeah, "slut" worked for both of them. She climbed his body, intent on only one thing. "Does that feel good? I want you to show me how good I make you feel."

With anyone else, that would be asking for fakey cries or theatrics, but this was Molly. That wasn't her style. Instead she pressed closer against him and looked him in the eyes. He felt her gaze in his balls, in the base of his pelvis like a sensuous caress. Her mouth was slightly open, her lips trembling with pleasure, but her eyes... He'd seen that look before. It was the look she used to give Clayton when they were in the club. Adoration, desire, and a kind of wonder that humbled him. Yes, he understood. He felt it too.

He buried his fingers in her hair and pressed his cheek to hers. His lips were poised at her ear, but all he could think to say was her name, over and over, like some mantra. The chair groaned beneath them as she orgasmed, and then it overturned, tumbling them both, still connected and still climaxing, to the floor.

Mephisto caught and cradled her, claiming her. Filling her with his cum. Molly laughed hysterically, her legs tangling with his. He felt in that moment so alive, so replete. Their eyes locked and Molly gave him a smile. Such a smile. He traced her lips, and then, somehow, she was smiling and crying at the same time.

Mephisto wiped away her tears. "What is it? What's wrong?"

"I want to belong to you," she said. "I've wanted it for so long. I'm ready now, if you'll have me. If you want all of me. If you want me to call you Master."

Mephisto's cock pulsed, still deep inside her, to hear the word Master on her lips. "You're sure?" he asked. "I want you to be sure, because I won't make it easy for you to back out again. Once you're mine..." He didn't complete the sentence. He didn't have to. Molly knew him well enough, remembered their history well enough to know what serving him would entail.

"I'm sure." Her voice was steady, and so was her gaze. "I'm ready if you want me. I've never been more sure of anything in my life."

CHAPTER NINE
MASTER

They didn't go to his bed, or to the club's dungeon play space. Not to the kitchen or Mephisto's makeshift office. They went out.

I'm ready if you want me, she had told him. *I've never been more sure of anything in my life.*

They were powerful words for both of them. Upon hearing them, Mephisto decided he needed air. Now there had to be some frank talk, some explicit negotiation, and the only place they could talk about those kinds of things without falling all over each other was out in the public eye. So they went to the park.

He sat on the grass, leaning back on his arms. Molly sprawled beside him with her head resting in his lap. Now and again he reached down to pet her, to stroke the glossy black waves of her hair. It was a beautiful fall day, with just the right amount of sunshine and breeze. He felt elementally relaxed, but Molly shifted now and again, as if she was already uncomfortable being clothed. When he'd made her dress again she'd done so with reluctance. He thought she probably would rather have had this discussion naked and locked in his cage. She'd told him she was ready, and he believed she was ready, but he would make her tread water just a little longer before he let her sink under the waves.

"So what made you decide it was time?" he asked. "Your meeting with Eliot?"

She thought a moment. "Maybe. I think squaring that away was always a natural transition point in my mind. But I wasn't really sure until I talked to him."

"Did you tell him who I am to you? About Club Mephisto?"

"Vaguely. He knows about Club Mephisto. I think he didn't want to know any more. And I didn't really want to get into it with him."

"He wouldn't have understood anyway."

Her eyes met his, so piercing blue in the sun. "Yes, exactly. But you understand. I think you understand me better than anyone else who's ever been in my life."

"Even your old Master?"

She didn't answer for a moment, only swallowed hard. Then she said, "Yes."

Mephisto missed Clayton. He'd respected Clayton as a dominant and as a man, but he thought Molly was probably right. She turned on her back, staring up at the sky, the fingers of one hand toying with the hem of his jeans. "Do you believe in heaven?" she asked. "An afterlife? All that stuff?"

"No, kitten," he said regretfully. "Do you?"

"No, but I wish I did. It just doesn't seem possible, that that's it. That once you're gone..."

Mephisto brushed a wisp of hair from her eyes. They were welling a little. "Is he really gone though? I remember him. You remember him. We talk about him a lot, and he affected both of us very deeply. That stays as long as we stay, you know?" There were tears now, quiet ones falling down her cheeks and onto his thigh. "Just so you know, that doesn't ever have to change. Clayton was a very special, unique part of your life. Even when you call me Master, there will still be room for him."

She blinked and swiped her tears away. "I don't know why I'm crying. He would have been happy today. I was just thinking, if I'm wrong and there is a heaven, he's probably looking down on us feeling pretty glad."

Mephisto smiled. "Yes, I think so. But cry all you want. We're both about to take a very important step, make a very important commitment. You're sure about this?"

She barely paused to think about it. "I'm sure. I trust you completely. I'm closer to you than anyone else on earth."

"But that doesn't mean you have to submit to me. We can have trust and closeness without deep slavery. We've already shown that, I think."

She took a while longer to mull over that. "Well..." She stuck out her tongue a little, and bit her lip. "I really want to do it for you."

"Why?"

"Because I know you want it, that you would enjoy it. And I like making you happy."

Her words were disturbing and lovely all at once. He brushed a thumb across her cheek. "You shouldn't do it for me. You should mostly do it for you."

She laughed and took his hand, and pressed her lips to his palm. "You know I want it ten times more than you do. You *know*."

Mephisto laughed too. He did know. He lay down on his side and put an arm around her waist, then slid lower so they were face to face. "You need to understand this though... I'm not Clayton Copeland. I'll demand service and sex and whatever else I enjoy from you, but there are things I won't do. I won't let you disappear. Do you know what I mean by that?"

She looked down at some point near the collar of his tee. "I'll have to keep doing my self-improvement afternoons?"

"And your volunteer mornings, yes. Until further notice. I know this will make you very busy, because you'll have to do other things for me too, but I like busy slaves." She was biting her lip again. "What? What is it?"

"Will I have to cook for you?"

"God, no. Not without cooking lessons first. And no ironing. Ever." He ran a hand over a faint scar on her forearm. "I know from personal experience that you and irons don't mix."

She gave him a shy, impish smile. "Maybe if I had lessons first."

"You're pressing your luck, little slave girl," he replied, gripping her wrist. Even that gentle, teasing bondage ignited a spark in her eyes, a hot resonance in her body. He groaned softly, too softly for her to hear. He had to get her home. Soon. But first...

"From here on out, I'd like you to call me Master." His voice was low and passionately intense. "I'll try to be a careful, nurturing Master to you. I won't offer you a collar for at least a month, so if things don't work out..."

He couldn't finish that sentence. Didn't really need to. They both knew things would work out. He cupped her face in his hands and kissed her lips, once, twice. He opened his eyes to find her gazing back at him, all there, all lucid, and happily choosing to submit to his will.

"You know," he said, "sometimes I'll want times like these when we just hang out. Not as Master and slave. As lovers. As friends. I'll want deep talks and long walks. I won't give you a full-time dynamic that never changes. Not because I don't value you, but because I value you too much. Do you understand what I'm saying?"

After a pause, she nodded. "Me and Clayton used to have times like that. Well, my collar never came off but..." She blinked a few times. "In the end, those are the times I really remember. Not because they were the best times between us, but because they were the times we felt most connected."

"It's weird but I almost always feel connected to you. I felt a connection the first time I saw you. Do you remember?"

She buried her head in his shoulder. "No. I was too drunk."

"You were drunk as a skunk, and I hate drunk ass people, so there was something else there. Something more that drew me to you."

She looked up at him, her eyes sharp with curiosity. "What was it? That something more?"

I burned for you. I've burned for you for so long. "I don't know. Some spark, Molly. With people like us, you can't always explain why you want something. You just do." He stroked her hair one more time and got to his feet, reaching down to help her up. "Come on, let's get some ice cream before we head back."

* * * * *

The ice cream was a nice touch. Molly remembered him feeding her an ice cream cone...oh...ages ago. Two and a half years ago, just like this, only then she'd been on the tail end of a really difficult week of orgasm denial and speech restriction, implemented by Mephisto, of course. She'd hated it in the moment, but later, she'd thought of it time and time again, and in hindsight it was nothing but hot. Scorching.

Things were still hot between them. Growing hotter. Mephisto licked her lips as often as he licked the ice cream cone. He stared as she ran her tongue up the mountain of vanilla soft-serve, teasing him. She ended up with some on her nose and he licked that off too. An older lady walking by gave both of them an affronted glare.

He leaned close, brushing warm lips against her temple. "Messy little girl," he said. "Where are your parents?"

Molly giggled. "They're not watching. They, uh...let me wander off."

"Did they?" He held the cone, urging her to take another lick. She could actually see his erection growing larger behind the fabric of his jeans. She swirled her tongue around the tip and waggled it at him. He sighed softly. "You're a bad girl, aren't you? They didn't let you wander off. You ran away."

Molly fluttered her eyes at him. "I'm not a bad girl. I'm a good girl. I'm a really good girl."

Mephisto stifled a smile as she did more obscene things to the ice cream cone, then he took another broad lick himself. Ohh... It reminded her of things. Naughty things. He eyed her and pulled her into his lap.

"If you come home with me, little girl, I'll give you candy."

"Candy?" Molly put a finger to her bottom lip. "But I'm not supposed to take candy from strangers."

"And toys. I can show you some toys you'll really love."

"You have toys?"

His gaze darkened. "I have lots of things for a good girl like you in my dungeo— At my house."

"It is a nice house?"

"A nice house?" Mephisto squeezed her. "It's made of gingerbread, with a candy roof."

Molly laughed and buried her head against his neck. He smelled like fresh air and vanilla ice cream. "Do you have room for me at your gingerbread house?"

He forced her head back and dropped a kiss on her lips. "I have plenty of room for a lost little girl like you. You need a place to call home, and a Daddy to make you behave better." His eyes glittered with a wicked spark. "I have a special cage with your name on it, and a pretty collar if you're good." He chuckled softly. "I had a chastity belt too, but a very bad girl I used to know shredded it and set it on fire."

She feigned horror, gasping, and then she laughed. She and her old Master had seldom joked and played like this. Mephisto was different, but that was okay. She was having fun. She felt safe. She shifted closer on his lap, leaning into his broad chest, knowing she'd made the right decision. After so many months of turmoil and uncertainty, she felt relaxed at last in his arms. In his care. As they split the last few licks, excitement started to flare in her middle. When he crunched through the last of the cone and looked down at her, she shivered.

"I hope you don't have any plans for the rest of the afternoon," he murmured, sliding his erection against her hip.

"I'm supposed to spend every afternoon doing something to improve myself," Molly said.

"Oh, I'll be improving you, kitten," he returned with a breathtaking smile. An alarming smile, really. The ride back home seemed to take a lot longer than the ride there. She was going to be his now. His to manipulate, to play with, to punish if he wished it. He'd so carefully adhered to her boundaries while she made her way through her confusion and sadness following her Master's death. Now she'd taken those boundaries away.

Oh my God. Oh, yes.

He stopped her just inside the door. "Clothes off. No more clothes in the house unless you're told to wear them." The corner of his mouth turned up slightly. "You're used to that, yes?"

She smiled. "Yes, Master. But it's been a while." Wow, over half a year. It seemed longer and yet it seemed like only moments had gone by.

"It will feel normal again soon," he said. "Go put your clothes in the bedroom, use the restroom, and return here."

Molly shot a look around the play space. It was dark even during daylight hours, by design of course. By the time she returned, the darkness was replaced by the glow of what had to be twenty or thirty candles placed in various places around the room. It was scary and eerie but so beautiful in a way. Like him.

He stood beside a bondage rack, his shirt off, his hands open at his sides. She swallowed hard and tried to present herself to him without feeling ashamed. Without feeling fearful. *I trust him. I do.*

"How sleek you look without your clothes on, kitten." His voice was low and smooth, the voice of someone comfortable being in charge. He beckoned her and she crossed to him like she was caught in some dungeon-based tractor beam. When she was near enough, he reached for her. He slid an arm around her waist, snaking the other hand down to cup her mons. "Such a pretty kitty," he murmured.

He parted her with his fingers. She stared at the line of his hard jaw as he probed and stroked between her slick pussy lips. It felt too good already. She wouldn't be able to focus on pleasing him if he visited this kind of pleasure on her. She moaned softly as heat throbbed like a drum in her center. Candlelight flickered off his smooth bronze skin and reflected in his dark eyes as he looked at her.

"You can beg for what you'd like, kitten. It would turn me on to hear it."

"Will you— *Ah...*" Her voice cut off as he finger fucked her even deeper. "Will you let me have the things I ask for, Master?" she asked shakily.

"Probably not. But I'll enjoy hearing you beg and whimper when you don't get your way."

His words settled right there in her clit, right there beneath his fingers, teasing her, tormenting her.

"Please, Master."

"'Please' is sweet but not specific enough. Tell me what you want."

"Please keep touching me. Please let me come," she burst out. "Please let me show you how much you're turning me on."

He chuckled. "Oh, I see. You'd be orgasming for my benefit, is that it?"

She shook her head, trying to concentrate over the building, rollicking hum between her legs. "I want whatever will bring you pleasure, Master."

"What if it will bring me pleasure to tie you to this rack here and mark you all over with a Plexiglass cane?"

She swallowed hard and made herself meet his gaze. "Then...then that's what I want." Her voice kind of cracked on the last word. "I want to please you, Master. However I can." *But please, please don't do that to me.* She had to get good again at silencing the inner dialogue that kept her from connecting fully with her Master. She had to get good at finding her slave-space, where even pain and challenge brought comfort.

Suddenly his light caresses ceased and he was in motion. He pulled her arms over her head and pushed her against the rack, which was a kind of iron lattice structure. He made her hold on to the nearly-uppermost bar, so she had to either stretch out or go up on her toes.

"Whatever you do, don't let go."

Molly sucked in a breath, her heart banging in her chest. It was so cruel to not actually bind her, tie her down. If only he'd done that, she could have let the ropes do all the work of submission. The ropes would have kept her standing there, forced to accept whatever he did to her. Without rope or cuffs, Molly had to find the will to submit somewhere within herself. She'd have to summon the will to hold on when every impulse would scream to let go and run to safety. She tightened her fingers on the metal bars as her Master moved to the wall of the play space. Her whole body felt hypersensitive. Her skin ached from the threat of waiting for pain. She rested her forehead against the bars in front of her, realizing that her pussy was as warm with lust as her body was cold with dread.

Like her old Master, Mephisto didn't give her any warnings, any explanation of what he'd do to her, how many strokes, with what. *I want whatever will bring you pleasure, Master.* She meant those words and she knew Mephisto understood they gave him the right to do just about anything to her. He returned and Molly didn't look back. She just waited, his willing victim.

Crack! The contact of the strap surprised her so much she almost let go. She'd expected the fire cut of the cane but instead got this intense, aching sting. It was a wide, thick strap and it fell twice more before the intensity of the ache really registered with her. *Whap, whap, whap...*more blows. Each time it connected with her ass, the pain burned more intensely. She made little cries and went up on her toes, trying to assuage the torment the only way she was allowed, by shifting and clenching her ass cheeks. If she moved any more she'd have to let go—

He snapped the strap hard against the top of her thighs and then she did let go, reaching back to rub the hot pain in shock for just a moment. "I'm sorry, Master," she said at once, replacing her hands, but they both knew sorry wouldn't be enough. He came to her and pulled her head back.

"What did I tell you, slave?"

"Don't let go," she breathed, panicking. "Master, you said, 'Whatever you do, don't let go.'"

"And what did you do?"

She burst into tears. "I let go. I'm sorry. Please forgive me."

"Are you out of practice, girl? Did you forget how hard it can be to obey your Master?"

"Yes," she sobbed. "Yes, I did. I'm sorry."

"Sorry doesn't really help me, but maybe some more practice will help you. I wasn't going to mark the back of your thighs, but now I think I will, so you can practice your control."

"Tha—Thank you, Master."

He ran a hand down over her hot ass cheeks, down to her sopping wet pussy. "And know this. If you let go again without permission, this hungry, horny little pussy is going to go unsatisfied. Master will take his pleasure and leave his little kitten in pain."

She flinched at the hardness in his eyes. Oh, God, if he didn't let her come after all this...that would be the most painful thing of all. "I won't let go, Master."

She sighed as he buried his face in her neck and nibbled softly at her pulse. "See that you don't," he muttered as he pulled away.

Molly held the bars in a death grip. She would have given anything to be restrained. This was a test. He was letting her know that if she wanted to be his slave, she had to submit—without coercion or restraint—to his pain. But the reward if she was successful... She shivered a little, thinking of Mephisto taking her with his hard cock, claiming her, proving his mastery over her.

Whack! Whack! Whack! Molly stood fast and held on for dear life. The backs of her thighs had always been the most sensitive part of her. Her old Master had figured that out and punished her there when he was most angry. Master Mephisto had to be figuring it out too. She wailed with each horrible searing stroke, praying it would be the last. She could have pleaded, begged for mercy, but it would have been pointless. Her shoulders ached and her fingers grew numb from holding on so tight. Molly let her body sag against the bars, let the hard metal hold her and soothe her against the pain from behind.

At last he stopped. Molly stood trembling. Dreading. He walked away, returned again. "Just a little more practice. Don't let go."

Molly braced, and now...now the cane came. The first stroke of fire across the backs of her thighs brought a soundless gape of her mouth. The second stroke, a piercing scream. Her entire body tensed with the effort to stand still, to not let go. Another stroke, another scream, and stuttering, halting breaths choking her throat. He tapped her ass with the wicked implement.

"Breathe. Deep breaths. I'm almost finished."

"Almost finished" ended up being three more strokes, delivered with maximum delay in between, so Molly had to wait, shaking and shuddering. She was almost to the point of begging for each stroke just to get them over with. When they would come, the whistling sound, the rustle of his movement had a nightmarish quality. After the last stroke, he put a hand at the middle of her back and rubbed lightly.

"Okay, you can let go for a minute, but don't move."

Molly released the bar and put her hands over her face, wiping away tears.

"No," he said. "Don't brush them away. I like to see them. Put your hands at your sides."

That made her cry more. She made fists at her sides, her palms sweaty and sore, but not as sore as the backs of her legs. Her Master still rubbed her back, watching her face.

"I like that you'll hurt for a while, every time you sit down. You have some pretty marks on the backs of your thighs. Some nice bruises, some lovely cane tracks. But I think before we finish, I should even you out a little. Make your ass hurt as bad as your legs. That would please me."

Molly sniffled and nodded. "Yes, Master." Punishment on her ass would feel like nothing after this. At his sign, she reached above her to grasp the bar again. It felt clammy and cold now. When the pain came, it was the strap again. She whimpered and tensed her ass cheeks. With a rush of breath, he dropped the strap and came to her. He pinched one of her nipples until she whined and then groped her mons again. She arched into his touch, desperate for pleasure. Desperate to be filled, taken.

"You're so wet," he sighed. "You love when Master hurts you, don't you?"

She nodded, tears still streaming down her face. She wasn't sure though, if they were tears of pain or tears of emotion.

"No nodding. Answer me," he said.

"Yes, Master, I love when you hurt me."

"Here. Let go." He pried away her death grip on the bars and then slapped the back of one tender thigh. "Part your legs. Wider." He made Molly spread her legs until he was satisfied, until she felt open and vulnerable and exposed, and then he pushed her hands back against the rack, to a lower bar this time. "Hold on. Don't let go."

Molly was dying of arousal. It was bad enough to stand and be punished, to be his body to decorate with marks. Now she was a sexual plaything, her legs spread at his command. Now, she couldn't pretend this wasn't about sex, about her being as turned on as him. She stood there, open, waiting, wet as a river. Empty and dying to be filled with Master's cock.

The strapping began again, hard blows falling on her ass cheeks. Now, in addition to not letting go, she had to hold this overtly sexual position, and not jump up or clench her legs together at each punishing, sharp strike. A few times he aimed so the edge of the strap licked around her pussy and the inside of her thighs. The second time he did that, she cried and she did start begging.

"Please...please, Master!"

"Please?" He pretended confusion. "Harder? Would you like to be strapped harder?"

"No, Master. Please! You're hurting me so much." Even as she said the words, she wanted to take them back. She was being a selfish, weak slave. He cracked her again, right across her backside.

"I'm hurting you because I want to. And because you need it. You know that." *Crack!* "Apologize for the whining."

"I'm sorry, Master," she sobbed. "Please hurt me as much as it pleases you."

"Thank you, I will." *Crack! Whack!* He rained down stinging slaps in succession until her whole ass felt like it was on fire. Had she thought the whipping on the back of her thighs was the bad thing? Because this was growing significantly worse. Still, she didn't dare complain again. Instead her begging turned inward. *Please, please, let this be over soon. Please let me endure this.* Just at her limit, just when she thought she would have to give up and break role and throw herself at his feet for mercy, he stopped.

"Good girl. Don't move."

Molly went limp, clinging to the bar. Her skin simmered. The aching throb in her ass and thighs bloomed to almost painful lust in her pussy. After he finished putting away the cane and strap, he came to stand behind her. She heard him unzip his jeans, heard the rustle of them falling to the floor. She couldn't even bear to look...she was that excited. Her legs were still spread, her pussy and ass waiting and available for him. Either one, either hole. She'd take him either place just for the relief of feeling him drive into her and give her some release.

From behind, he poked his cock against her slippery center. Teasing, just teasing. She moaned and arched back to him. He chuckled, squeezing her sore ass cheeks. She felt humiliated but she didn't care. He moved behind her and his cock poked against the soreness of her punished flesh. She was still, letting him hurt or please her as he willed.

"Good girl," he repeated, more warmly this time. "Don't let go." His hands slid up her waist, then higher to cup her breasts. He squeezed them, capturing the tight peaks between his fingertips and hurting her again. Oh, God, it felt so good.

"Please. Please, Master," she whispered very quietly. Maybe it was just her lips moving, forming the words. *Please, please, please.*

He'd spread his legs too, so he was down on level with her. He used the extra leverage to impale her quickly and brutally on his cock. Well, it would have been brutal except that she was so prepared for him. He slid through her juices until he was balls deep, and then he was fucking her hard, grasping her hips and riding her like a toy. Each stroke was heaven to Molly. He ground against her g-spot as he drilled into her sensitive pussy lips.

She braced against the bar as his thrusts quickened. He was using her, marking her. This was a celebration of her surrender to him and their joy. Joy that they fulfilled each other, that they were so perfectly matched. His cock seemed to swell in her, so every movement was more ecstasy, more shimmering sensation. "Master, please, may I come? Your cock feels so good inside me."

"Yes, you can come." His words came out in a guttural grunt. "Let Master feel how thankful you are to be taking his cock. Let me feel it."

She contracted around his pounding shaft, his force and grasping hands spinning out the release, fanning the flames so the climax went on and on. She was so far gone she barely registered his own completion. He pressed against her back and held her hard, thrusting so deeply her feet were lifted from the floor. His lengthy, shuddery groan pretty much summed up her feelings at the moment. Even when he relaxed, he didn't let her go. She drifted, his body a firm, reassuring wall behind her.

"Oh, Master," she whispered.

"Oh, Jesus," he replied, slipping away from her with a sigh. Molly hated the feeling of emptiness left behind. She didn't want this scene to end. They'd played many times in the last few months but this was the first scene where he'd treated her like his slave, taking what he wanted, making her endure more than she thought she could take. She feared the moment when he'd leave her, when he released her from his control. She'd just found her way back to this place she lived for, and she didn't want to leave it yet.

Her Master crouched and turned her face to his, stroked her still-slightly-damp cheek. His gaze searched her features. She tried to compose her face into some semblance of servitude or submission, but she was still a mess. Still breathless, still aching for his closeness. Whatever he saw, it seemed to please him. He nodded at her hands.

"You can let go now."

She hadn't realized she was still grasping the bars. Her legs were still spread too, her whole body locked in the position he'd placed it in. When she let go of the bars she didn't know where to put her hands. *Wake up, girl. Snap out of it.* She clasped them in front of her, then spread them on his chest when he hauled her up against him. He licked one cheek, then kissed her on both eyes with light, breathy kisses. He drew her closer and plundered her mouth, one hand twisting in her hair.

He pulled away as suddenly as he engaged her and the corner of his mouth twitched in what might have been the ghost of a satisfied smile.

"What a good slavegirl you are. I enjoyed marking you and fucking you, and coming deep inside you."

"Yes, Master," she said when he looked at her expectantly. "I'm thankful that I pleased you."

He still watched her. She trembled a little. Before, they'd do a scene and he'd let her go. She didn't want to go now. She wanted his control around her like a shield, like a blanket keeping her warm a little longer. She knew she couldn't expect constant control from him. Even her old Master had gone off to work and left her to her own devices much of the day.

"I think I'll put you in the cage for a little while," he finally said. "You can rest and think about how much your ass and legs ache. Would you like that?"

She knew the question was rhetorical, that he would do as he liked, but she automatically answered "Yes, Master."

"And you can think about Master fucking your ass later, just before dinner, and how sore you'll be sitting on your spanked, fucked ass while we eat. I think I'll make it a real ass-reaming," he mused, ostensibly to himself. Molly tensed in delicious anticipation and fear.

"Yes, Master. Whatever you wish."

"Well, go on. Back to my room."

He offered her his arm to steady her. Her legs still weren't working quite right yet, or maybe they were already trembling over what was coming next. Molly had been great at anal sex when she'd been a full time slave but she'd have to get back into practice now. Somehow she knew Master Mephisto would make it his immediate mission to bring her up to speed.

In his room she walked to the familiar, large cage in the corner. It was lined with blankets so it wasn't like lying on the hard floor, but it wasn't exactly a cozy haven either. She crawled into the enclosure, curling up on her side since she couldn't stretch out straight.

"Oh, no," Mephisto said. "On your back. I want you to feel that sore ass while you're thinking about what's coming." He reached in and tapped her thigh. "Legs spread too."

She drew in a breath and complied, her completely satiated body now betraying her by getting white-hot horny again. She looked over at her Master, let him see her frustration—and her arousal. His only answer was pleased laughter.

"You little wanton. Don't dare think of passing the time in there playing with your wet, hungry pussy. There will be times I'll make you do that so I can watch, but this is not one of those times." He indicated a small camera set into the ceiling. "Behave."

"Yes, Master." Molly shifted her hips forward a little and then resigned herself to lying on her sore ass until...well...until he came for her.

It was deliciously simple in a way. Deliciously sexy. She was his captured, thrilled slave, completely at his mercy. It was exactly what she craved.

CHAPTER TEN
TOGETHER

Mephisto forced himself from the room, forced himself back out to the play space where he could think again. He drifted around putting out candles, remembering her softly spoken words.

I want to please you, Master. However I can.

He'd almost splooged right in his jeans when she said that, only because he understood she meant it. Even without her wide expressive eyes, the sincerity in her voice...he knew. Other slaves could talk as prettily as Molly, but with them it was posturing. Play. Molly *meant* it, even as tears had gathered in her eyes at the thought of being tortured with the cane.

As if. As if he could have punished her so harshly after that heart—and cock—wrenching display of submission to his will.

Now his obedient, beautiful slave was stored away, more for her protection than anything else. He'd been ready for round two about three seconds after round one was over, but he demanded the same control of himself that he demanded of her. He would have torn her ass up with the wildness he felt at that moment. Anyway, it was better for both of them to wait, to anticipate. He went to his desk and glanced at the monitor window open on his computer screen. She was still on her back, her legs still spread to his specifications. Ah, God, it was so goddamn hard to wait.

Every so often she stretched and braced her legs against the bars, but even then she kept her thighs spread. That was the kind of slave she was. She would sooner maim herself than disobey. It was a virtue—but also a danger. It was the reason it would have been really hard for Mephisto to entrust her into another Master's care, even though he'd thought many times of who he could steer her toward if she wouldn't agree to be his. Fortunately he wouldn't have to do that any longer. Clayton had struggled with the same fear, Mephisto knew. He'd thought about Clayton a lot today. Clay would have been happy to know how things panned out.

Mephisto looked over his digital to-do list. At the bottom he added *Collar for Molly*. After a moment he also typed *Chastity belt?* He looked over at Molly on the cam again and deleted the chastity belt note. Eventually, yes. At the moment, no. Hell no. So many other pleasures to enjoy for now. After he enjoyed conquering her little asshole, it would be time for dinner, and then Club Mephisto's employees would start arriving. Patrons would fill his club, set about driving one another wild, but Mephisto had a feeling he would still be thinking about Molly.

He decided he would make her lie under his desk that night during club hours, perhaps even blindfold her. When he craved her, when he needed release, he'd go sit at his desk and she could service him, hidden from view. Ah, that was hot and she would love it. Maybe he'd put her in a double dildo harness and let her finger herself while she sucked his cock. If she could bring herself off before he finished, he'd give her some reward above and beyond a mouthful of his cum...

His sexual imagination was endless. His patience was not. He got so rigid imagining scenarios that any further work became impossible. He stood and stalked to the bedroom. As soon as he entered, Molly's eyes latched onto his, then dropped to his engorged, jutting cock. *Yes, little kitten, this is going in your ass shortly. Like, a minute from now.* He was still every bit as naked as she was, which was fortuitous, since in its rock solid state, his cock might have busted right though the denim of his jeans.

He crossed the room and yanked the cage door open, pulled his slave out, and bent her over the bed. It occurred to him perhaps he should have prepared her with a plug first, made her wear it while she waited in the cage. But then, she would enjoy this more if it hurt a little. He let her wait while he crossed to the bureau to grab a condom. He added just a thin sheen of lube to what was already there and ogled her ass and thighs as he returned to stand behind her. Beautiful marks, and they would deepen by tomorrow.

He grabbed a cheek in each hand and squeezed hard, kneading her bruises. She groaned and ground her hips against the edge of his bed.

"Give me your hands." His sharp request sounded suspiciously like a snarl. "Put them behind you."

She reached back and he circled her wrists, holding them tight in one fist. With the other hand, he pressed the head of his shaft against her little, spasming hole.

"You won't make this difficult for Master, will you?" he asked with an edge of warning. "I don't want to force my way in, but I will if I have to."

She whimpered, her legs tensing. He pressed her hands down firmly at the small of her back and eased partway in. Good God, she was so hot, so tight. An animal sound tore from his throat, pent up desire finally released. She stretched around him, her body quivering as she struggled to accommodate his size. She made quiet sounds of distress, but nothing dire enough to make him retreat.

"Good girl. Good girl..." he crooned softly. "Be a good girl and take Master's fat cock in your ass. It feels good, doesn't it?"

"Yes...Yes, Master," she gasped through tightly clenched lips.

"Beg for me to go deeper."

"Master, please, fuck me deeper!"

"Beg for me to drive in all the way," he said, squeezing her wrists when she fidgeted under him. "Beg me to fuck you hard."

"Please, Master, drive in me all the way, balls deep. Fuck me hard, even if it hurts me."

He slapped her ass, causing her ring to clench around the head of his cock. "I won't hurt you too badly, kitten. But I'll hurt you enough to show you who's in charge."

He slid deeper, the sadist in him thrilling to the sound of her drawn out hiss. She went up on her toes as he bottomed out in her, the lube on the condom only slightly smoothing the way. He sawed out and in again, bumping his hips against her red ass. Finally he felt her relax and accept him. When he could enter and leave her with less resistance, he increased his pace, drilling her, feeling a delicious, brutal tension swirl in his balls. Assfucking offered so many pleasures. The tightness, the resistance, and the fact that it was nearly impossible to assfuck a woman without tumbling her down into a submissive place.

Mephisto groaned and spread Molly's legs even wider with a nudge of his knees. Her little pain-and-lust noises were driving him wild. He noticed with amusement that she was grinding unabashedly against the edge of the mattress now. The insistent swivel of her hips was the perfect complement to the friction of him driving in and out. "Don't come yet," he warned her. He could come any time—she turned him on that much— but he'd promised her an ass-reaming and that was what she was going to get. "I'll tell you when you can come. Don't come before or you'll be sorry."

Ah, sweet little thing wasn't grinding anymore. Smart slave. He pushed her hands up by the back of her neck, and without instruction she laced them there at her nape. He grabbed her hips and fucked her for long moments...fast, slow, hard, harder, and then gently, sliding in and out so sensually that she gripped every inch. As his slave, she would have to take his cock in her ass whenever the mood struck him, which would be a lot. Best that she get comfortable with that reality.

He fucked her until she started to zone out, and then he let go of her hips and ran his fingers up her back. He grabbed her hands and pinned them to the bed on either side of her head, leaning over her, driving deep. Her wedding rings from Clayton still shone on her finger. It didn't bother him at all. *Clay, man, I can't thank you enough for this.* "Are you ready to come with Master's cock deep in your ass?"

"Yes. Yes, Master!"

She arched back against him and those little hips started bucking and grinding again. He could have helped her, spread her pussy lips and fingered her clit—he knew exactly where to touch her and how hard—but it amused him more to make her work for it, arching helplessly in the space between his hips at her back and the edge of the bed pressed against her front. She started to moan, her ass twitching around his cock. It didn't seem possible for him to get any harder but in that moment he did. The tingling became a roar, the steady drive a necessity. He slid into her with all the ungoverned desire he felt, bearing her down hard into the bed, and then she was writhing under him, crying out in ecstasy. She clamped down in a rhythmic, powerful orgasm around the base of his cock, and with a howl, he let loose inside her.

Holy fuck. He was going to crush her, but he couldn't draw back, couldn't control the impulse to drive in her, to empty out all the excitement and pleasure she built up in him. When his climax subsided, when the blood stopped beating in his ears, he raised himself off her enough to let her take a breath. He was still gripping her hands. He turned one and kissed the palm, then the other, and returned her hands to the bed, where they rested, limp and half open. He pulled out and took off his condom, then returned to find her still sprawled, legs wide open. He nudged against her with one knee.

"Are you alive, or should I notify your next of kin?"

"I am..." She paused. "I am barely alive, Master." She made a sound that he wanted to remember forever. A thrilled, exhausted, delighted sound. He helped her up and swept her into his arms, just because he wanted to hold her in that moment, clasp all her sweetness and beauty right against his chest. She shrieked and grabbed at his shoulders.

"I won't drop you, kitten, don't worry. Although I'm sure you'd land on your feet."

He took her to the shower and scrubbed her up, allowing her to do the same for him, and then they went to the kitchen to eat and prepare for the night ahead. Mephisto decided he wouldn't force Molly to appear out in the club, not yet, but he gave her the choice. She decided she would come play for a little while, although she looked uneasy about it.

"Do you not want to come because you think I might play with someone else? Will it bother you if I do?" he asked.

Molly took a long time to answer. "It would bother me terribly, Master, because I'm jealous and I don't want to share you with anyone. But the choice is yours. If that's what you need to be happy, I'll learn to live with it."

Like the cane. Like the chastity belt in her future, and all the torments he'd dream up for her. She'd live with them because she'd agreed to be his slave. But lucky for her, emotional torture had never been his speed.

"I doubt I'll take any other slaves for a while," he said, reaching across the table to take her hand. "I have a feeling you'll keep me satisfied enough on your own."

* * * * *

Over the next few weeks, Mephisto's life sorted into a relaxing, fulfilling balance of work and playing with Molly every chance he got. It wasn't always easy. At his insistence, she kept up her forays into the outside world, her volunteerism and adventures in self-improvement. She surprised him in her creativity—and her persistence. Her involvement in charities started to rival Clayton's old habit of really getting in there and trying to improve the world from the ground up. Mephisto found himself attending playground openings, working on Habitat for Humanity sites, and, awkwardly, reading to children at the hospital. Well, he was awkward at it, but Molly was amazing. She spent every Wednesday morning at the pediatric hospital, and all the kids adored her and clambered to sit in her lap, to talk to her and tell her their stories.

Molly would have made a wonderful mother.

Damn Clayton for taking that out of the picture for her. Well, it wasn't totally out of the picture. They could adopt. They could easily adapt their dynamic to make room in their lives for a child. But when Mephisto tried to talk to Molly about kids, about how good she was with them, hinting at deeper possibilities, she clammed up. It was clearly a sensitive topic for her. He wondered if she regretted getting sterilized for Clayton. Really, Mephisto couldn't imagine himself as a father, even though he was nearing forty. Eternal hedonist. But if Molly really wanted kids...

Then again, they were barely getting used to being a couple. If they were going to get into conversations about that, it would be better to wait two or three more years. Maybe five years.

But she looked so sweet with those kids.

Aside from her charity work, there were ongoing legal duties she had to attend to, issues having to do with Clayton's estate. She attended these meetings alone, dressed in her smart little business suits and low heeled pumps. Mephisto didn't understand how the men who attended these meetings managed not to fall on her and rape her under the table. But they didn't, so Mephisto fell on her and raped her at home. Well, he didn't rape her, but he definitely ripped her smart little business suits off with a lot of gusto and fucked her across the floor with her stockinged legs sliding across his back. He never punished her when her smooth leather pumps kicked him involuntarily when she came.

He very simply craved her all the time. He'd wait, counting the moments even as he busied himself with the necessary tasks of running his business. No matter if she returned from the gym, or violin lessons, or some meditation workshop, he was there waiting for her, to strip off her clothes and reclaim her. He shared her with the outside world only reluctantly, but he had to do it because he wouldn't enjoy Molly's submission at her own expense.

He questioned her one day about her environmental science degree, asked her if she wanted to use it to go back to work in her field. She didn't, but she'd already started following environmentally responsible companies and investing heavily in them with Clayton's money. She did all these powerful and amazing things, his delectable little slave, and then she came home to him and served him, and he knew that service was what fulfilled her most of all.

He wasn't misguided enough to believe he had anything to do with that, beyond being judged worthy enough to receive her service. Molly's needs and talents were inborn. Like him, she'd felt a fascination with power exchange long before she understood about relationships and sex. She told him funny stories of tying herself up as a child, forcing herself to wait in a dark closet even though she was afraid. *I'm glad you're here to do it for me now,* she'd sigh, as he tied her or whipped her. No dark closet, but a cage she spent time in nearly every day. Mephisto knew she'd be perfectly content to sleep in there, but most nights he wanted her with him, so in that, she didn't get her way.

When it seemed she was sinking into life as his slave quite blissfully, when it seemed a sure, longtime thing, he started searching in earnest for a collar for her. Lorna was his go-to source for leather and harnesses, but for jewelry he turned to his friend Tadpole, a 50ish metalworker gentleman whose amphibious name was never explained. His name didn't matter. All anyone cared about was that he made the most beautiful jewelry, collars, manacles, and piercings to be found. Mephisto decided he wanted something delicate and decorative for Molly. Something she could wear every day without fielding inappropriate questions, but something with a weight and design that would remind her of her status, and something strong enough to be yanked on when he was feeling that way.

Tadpole finally came up with a stainless steel chain that would be sized to lie just at the base of her neck. It was thick enough to feel heavy, thick enough to provide the needed strength, but still delicate enough to pass for a necklace. On a whim Mephisto added a charm with the letter "M". Her outside friends and acquaintances would assume it stood for Molly, but Molly would know exactly what it stood for. Master, or Mephisto. Both. He was both things to her and hopefully would be for some time.

Good, she was finally home. He turned to her, taking in her sweet smile, her pretty curls. He didn't have to tell her what to do by this point.

She undressed with just a look from him, went to drop her clothes off in the laundry room. She returned and presented herself to him, chin up, hands at her sides.

"What did you do today, kitten?" he asked.

He half listened to her retelling. Family Center volunteering and lunch with Eliot—cleared with him first, of course. Eliot was apparently applying to law schools, mulling which branch of law he wanted to go into. Not surprisingly, Molly was nudging him toward environmental law. Mephisto thought the hapless man would probably end up doing it, because Molly was hard to say no to, even with her soft voice and self-effacing manner. Anyone who really knew her knew the strength that lied beneath. After that, in the afternoon, spa treatment and waxing. He smiled and palmed her smooth mons.

"What a fun, relaxing day for you," he murmured.

"Not totally fun, Master. A woman came into the Family Center today. She had been...terribly..." His slave's voice tensed up, and tears pooled in her eyes. "And she had this...this little girl..."

"Oh, honey." He pulled her close and embraced her, letting her feel the safety she craved, the safety she wished for everyone. He had a feeling there'd been some very dark days in her own childhood, only because she never, ever talked about her past with him. "It's good that she came in to get some help," he said. "Now she and her daughter can be safe."

"No," Molly said into his shoulder. "She left her daughter and went back to her husband. She said he loved her, and she loved him. But she worried for her daughter."

Mephisto just held her. This wasn't the first sad story she'd told him from the Family Center, and undoubtedly wouldn't be the last. She pulled back and looked at him. "I'm so thankful for you. That you're not like that. That I can trust you." Her eyes took on a faraway look. "But I wonder what will end up happening to that little girl."

He stroked her hair, brushed away the one fat tear that escaped. "With any luck, she'll find her way to a safe place."

After a moment, Molly seemed to master her emotions. She forced a smile and held his hand. "Master, I missed you. How can I serve you? I've been looking forward to serving you all day."

He guided her to her knees and unzipped himself. She attended to him with the expertise and attention of a seasoned slave, while he tried not to collapse under the continuous waves of pleasure. She licked and fondled him, taking his cock deep when he grasped the back of her neck. "Yes...yes," he moaned. "Such a good girl."

Before he was too far gone, he stopped her, pulled her up and backed her over to medical-play table. He strapped her ankles into the stirrups and forced her thighs wide. He loved to lick her pussy, partly because he knew she hated it and partly because he loved her softness and her taste. "Please, no," she begged. Molly's pussy and clit were so sensitive that Mephisto's teases and nibbles were like a form of torture to her. She wailed when he worked his tongue all around her clitoral hood and lapped at the little button inside. "Master!"

She knew he wouldn't stop. He never stopped until she was so wrung out and overstimulated that she ceased to fight him, and then he'd part her legs and fuck her until she arched up off the table and yanked at the cuffs holding her down. Today there was a heightened feel to their joining, a deeper emotion. All this time he'd been preparing to collar her, he knew what he was really preparing for was sharing the revelation that he loved her, that he'd loved her for ages.

He was completely, desperately in love with her.

"Yes, kitten, yes."

She reached out for him as climax rolled over both of them. Afterward, lazily, he undid the cuffs and draped her legs over his shoulders, rubbing his hands across her sweet belly, so flat and yet femininely rounded at the same time. Her hips, her breasts, all of her so precious and lovely to him.

He told her over dinner, over chicken parm and salad with his favorite dressing he'd taught her to make. "I think it's time for us to become a little more permanent," he said. "I want you to wear my collar. Do you think you're ready for that?"

Molly gave him her sweet little smile. "I would love that, Master. You honor me so much."

"No, I love you so much." There, he'd said it. "I've actually loved you forever. A long time, anyway. This is long overdue. So if you're willing, I'll put a collar on you this weekend. A nice metal one that will never come off. Well, almost never. Would you like that, kitten?"

"Oh, Master." That was all she had to say, all she seemed capable of saying. From the joy in her eyes, he could tell the answer was yes.

CHAPTER ELEVEN
LUCKY

Molly cradled the violin beneath her chin, painstakingly tuning the instrument. All around her, granite tombstones stood at attention, her captive audience, but she was playing for one man and one man only. Clayton Copeland, resting under the ground.

Other than the tombstones, the cemetery was empty. There was only Master Mephisto, sitting a few rows away on a scrolled iron bench. He always let her and Clayton have their privacy, but he wouldn't let her come alone. The cemetery was too isolated, he said. Maybe, in the beginning, he'd worried that she wouldn't come home, that she'd do something drastic here. She'd thought about it many times the first few weeks. She'd spent hours sobbing her eyes out and clawing at the ground like she could get at the man who'd deserted her, the man she'd loved and hated at once.

"This is from a Bach sonata in C-minor," she said in the silence. "I've been practicing it for a while."

She stood in front of his headstone and played the pretty, somewhat mournful melody. She played it because it was beautiful, and because she'd worked a long time to get to a point where she was proud to play for him, even though he couldn't hear it. The tone of her violin was almost perfect, post-repair, but not quite. That was okay with her. In one thoughtful moment it had occurred to her that the violin was like her and her old Master's relationship. Almost perfect, but not quite. It didn't make it any less worthwhile to her. Someone could come pry her imperfect violin away from her cold dead hands if they wanted to try it. She wouldn't let it go, and she'd never let Clayton go either, not while she drew breath.

Luckily Master Mephisto was okay with that. From her peripheral vision she could see him sitting, watching, waiting for her. This wasn't the first time she'd played at her former Master's gravesite. She'd started doing it several weeks ago, back when she and Mephisto were living together but not yet as Master and slave. Back when she'd been seeing Eliot and feeling conflicted about her needs. Clayton hadn't had any answers for her then, and he didn't now, but it brought her a great sense of connection to play for him here.

When she finished the short sonata she stretched her fingers and looked up at the sky. It was a bright, sunny blue even though winter was approaching. It had been cold when Clayton died, and it had upset her, thinking of him lying in the cold ground. It would grow cold again, and again, and again, year after year. She knew he couldn't feel it but the idea of it still chilled her.

"This is the second half of Bach's Chaconne. I'm not that good at it yet but I'll try for you. Bach wrote it for his wife after she died." She lifted her bow, then stopped. "It's not maudlin though. Just beautiful. I think you'll like it. And I'll keep practicing, and I'll come here and play it again for you in a year and you'll see how much better I am."

She began to play. After a few bars she glanced over to find Master Mephisto watching her directly now. If he thought she was crazy for talking to ghosts and gravestones he kept it to himself. Chaconne was a lengthy piece, but wonderful to play. She liked the second half especially. While Molly made a few mistakes, she enjoyed filling the quiet cemetery with music on this clear, blue-sky day. When she finished, she knelt to place her violin in its case.

She crept closer to his headstone then, tracing the letters of his name, the dates of his birth and death. *Husband and friend*, it read, a simple epitaph for a very rich and powerful man. They were his own words, laid out in his explicitly framed funeral plans. In Molly's mind, it should have been *Husband, Master, and friend*, but she understood why that wouldn't have worked. Below there was a small etched heart—a space, she was told, for her own name and dates if she chose to be buried here. That at least was appropriate, that her heart would reside there forever beneath his name, even if, for some reason, she didn't sleep here someday.

She raised her eyes to Master Mephisto, then lowered them again.

"Master, you should know..." She reached out and ran her fingers over the grass at the base of the stone, over the fresh, dewy flowers she always brought to decorate his grave. "You should know that your friend Mephisto is going to collar me. Soon. Tomorrow I think."

Last night she'd crept into the closet in the guest room, huddled against her Master's pillow and grasped his eternity collar against her chest and sobbed for him. Sobbed for the end of them. Mephisto had come to her and told her what she already knew, that there were no endings. That going to Master Mephisto didn't mean losing Master Clayton, or betraying him, or losing faith. Later, her old Master visited her in her dreams. He'd come before, but this time it felt so real. He'd come to her warm and naked, and pressed his body to hers. He'd worn that smile she used to live for, his light blue eyes twinkling, communicating desperately needed approval. The familiar girth and length of his cock had pressed against her belly as he kissed her. "My darling girl," he'd said. "I'll always love you. Always, always, your whole life. I want you to be happy. Are you happy?"

"I am happy," she answered him now. "If you're somewhere listening to me, or in some spirit world somewhere, just know that I'm happy and that you were right all along. Master Mephisto is caring and wonderful, and I feel like he's just right for me. Not that we're very much like you and I used to be."

She bit her lip and sniffled a little, tears coming to her eyes.

"Sometimes I wonder at some of the stuff you did. But I'm not mad. I was different then. I know you really cared for me and loved me in your way. I think maybe you were what I needed then, but Master Mephisto is who I need now, so I hope you're happy for us." She smiled, touching his name again. "I know you meant all along for me to be his if anything happened to you. Anyway..."

She stood up and brushed at her knees. "I'll come again soon. Next time I'll show you my collar. He says it's a chain this time, and it's pretty, although yours was pretty too. I still have it. I'll always keep it." She paused, crouching and reaching down to touch the heart, her heart. "I miss you so much, Master. I love you. I always will."

She straightened and looked over at Mephisto. He stood from his shady bench and came to join her. "You okay?"

He always asked that, and she always did feel surprisingly okay. She nodded and picked self-consciously at her violin case.

"How's Clayton these days? Did you tell him about the collar?"

"Yes." She smiled. "He said he approves. He wants me to be happy."

"He always wanted you to be happy. Want me to carry that for you?"

She shook her head and clasped her violin case close as they started back to the car.

"Those songs you played were really beautiful, kitten. You've come a long way. I'm proud of you. He would have been too."

"Thank you, Master," she said softly. She didn't know if she was thanking Mephisto, or Clayton, or both of them. In the end, it probably didn't matter. Both of them had her heart.

* * * * *

Mephisto didn't want some big ceremony for his slave's collaring. Some rite or ritual, a lot of formal words. None of that was necessary.

No. On Sunday morning, after she took care of her personal needs, he simply tied her to his bed and started playing with her. He left some slack for her hands so she could struggle a little, but he tied her ankles more tightly. He didn't want her to have any sense of being able to close her legs. *Mine. All mine.*

He teased her mercilessly for an hour to begin. He clamped her nipples so her face grew tight with pain, then set a vibrator against her clit until her hips started to jerk. Just when her breathing reached a certain point, he'd shut the vibrator off. Clamps off. Breathe. Tease. Different clamps on again. Riding crop to the clit, tawse to the nipples. Vibrator, crying, pleading for mercy, for release.

But no, not yet. They stopped for breakfast, which for Molly consisted of a throat full of semen. Mephisto enjoyed toast and eggs, feeding Molly now and again once she was done sucking his cock. She squirmed in her place at his feet—he told her she was too horny to sit at the table. When he ordered her to sit still, the fun really began. She was clearly ready to jump out of her skin, but she controlled herself, clasping her hands tightly in her lap. The only indication of her need was the fierce lust in her gaze.

After breakfast he put her to work cleaning up the dishes while he prepped a generously sized ass plug and returned to where she stood at the sink. "Bend over."

She barely glanced back, just obeyed. Even the pain of the large intrusion in her asshole didn't seem to take the edge off her horniness. She pressed her hips against the edge of the countertop as he drove it home, sighing when it was fully seated. He lifted her, signaling her to finish the dishes. She moved gingerly now, her ass cheeks clenched as he shadowed her around the kitchen.

"Does that hurt, Molly? Having that big plug in your ass?" he asked.

She swallowed hard, placing the last dish in the dish rack. "It hurt going in, Master. Very much. It only hurts a little now."

"If you want my collar, you'll have to let me hurt you whenever I want to. That's something I require."

"Yes, Master."

"Do you want my collar, Molly?"

She turned to him, her eyes wide, her body open to him. "Oh, yes, Master. I want it more than anything on earth."

He took her to the dungeon space next, fixed her to a spanking trestle with her ass in the air, legs spread and secured at ankle and knee so she couldn't move. More nipple clamps, the chain between them wrapped beneath the apparatus so any jerks upward would result in a vicious yank. She spent another hour here, suffering for his pleasure. He beat her until her tears were real, until her cries grew desperate, and then he'd take a break, remove the clamps, let her think her ordeal was over, only to begin again once she calmed down. The lesson here: *I'll hurt you, sometimes very badly, but never beyond what you can take.*

It fascinated Mephisto to watch her body process the pain, and to watch the processes of her mind as well. At the end, he added pleasure into the mix, removing the clamps for good and sliding a vibrating wand beneath her pussy. How quickly her misery transformed into bliss. He knew that for Molly misery and bliss were tethered together on a very short line. He picked up a cane and marked her with it, hitting her harder than she probably could have taken at the beginning of the hour. It was just hard enough to keep her burgeoning orgasm at bay. Every time she ground on the wand, he lashed her again. She'd howl and shudder, and seek the pleasure to help her endure the pain.

"Okay, enough," he said, pulling the wand away mid-grind. Molly sobbed, her hips seeking solace that was no longer there. He gave her three more with the cane, accompanied by cries and yowls. By the last, she collapsed against the trestle, all pleasure fled from her body's memory, chased out by burning agony. He put away the cane and stood back to study her nicely marked ass and thighs. Satisfied, he crossed to the front of her.

"Why does Master hurt you?" he whispered.

"Because you're a sadist," she answered shakily. "My pain brings you pleasure, Master."

"That's right. Anyone who wants my collar has to be a masochist. Are you a masochist, Molly?"

"Yes, Master."

He slapped her fresh cane tracks. She threw her head back and made a desperate sound. "You want my collar?"

"Yes, Master. Please!"

Back to the bedroom. Unplugged, given a bathroom break. He put a swipe of tingling oil over her clit, ignoring her whispers for mercy, then tied her on her tummy with orders not to grind against the bed. He left her alone a while to struggle, to crave with her legs spread, her orifices open and needy. Surely she wished to grind her way to orgasm. Her body must want to take over at this point. It had to be a mind-over-matter thing for her. He could see the concentration on her face more than the tension in her body.

At last he approached again, knelt behind her and rolled on a condom. Even after the plug, her hole was a tight fit, but he pressed ahead nonetheless, slowly and firmly, and seated himself balls deep. Her fingers clenched the covers and a tear or two squeezed from her eyes as he fucked her roughly, mechanically. Another lesson. *You're my toy, my fuck doll when I want you to be. It's not about you, it's about my needs.* She wasn't crying from pain. She was crying from sexual frustration.

"I know," he said as he drilled her. "I know you want to come, don't you, baby?"

"Yes, Master."

"If you want to wear my collar, you'll only be allowed to come when I want you to. I might make you go weeks, months without orgasm. Do you still want to wear my collar, Molly?"

"Yes, Master."

Mephisto chuckled inwardly. Her answer was a lot slower in coming that time. She was probably thinking, *months?* It was only an exaggeration on his part, but he was glad to know she believed him capable of such horrible depravity. A month, indeed. Five days had almost killed both of them last time he tried a denial regimen with her. Thinking back to those delicious scenes, to their erotic history, had him fucking hard and fast to a mind-splitting orgasm. Fireworks went off behind his eyes as he buried himself in her ass and pressed her sore cheeks together, savoring every inch of her tightness. He looked down at her, wondering how close she was to orgasm. One easy way to tell. He slid a finger down the front of her waist to her mons, almost to her clit, then stopped. She made a sound he didn't think he'd ever heard a human make before. Yeah. Still pretty close.

He moved away to throw out his condom and untie her. She still looked hopeful, like now he might let her come, or give her the collar already, the collar she wanted so badly. Months without orgasm. Hm. He cleaned her up instead and led her to the cage in the corner, guided her in. "You know how this goes. On your back, legs spread. No touching, no coming." He shut the door and locked it, holding her woebegone gaze. "Oh, and I expect you to think about one thing and one thing only until I return to you. Master's cock filling your holes. Mouth, ass, pussy, whatever strikes your fancy, but that's what I expect you to do. Do you understand me?"

Molly looked like she was about to start bawling. "Yes, Master. It will give me a lot of pleasure to think about your cock."

"I hope so."

He left her, pretending not to hear the long suffering sigh she exhaled as he walked away. Out in his office he watched her on cam, squirming, taking deep breaths in and out, but never once closing her legs. What a good girl. What a good slave, and all his.

After twenty minutes or so he couldn't wait anymore. He grabbed the silver chain collar with its little "M" charm and returned to the bedroom. He hunkered down beside the cage, expecting perhaps irritation or agony, but her face lit up in a smile.

"I've been thinking about you, Master. Dreaming about you, waiting for you, and here you are."

He could have switched the words around and they would have worked as well. *I've been thinking about you, Molly. Dreaming about you, waiting for you, and here you are. My slave that I've waited for forever. Finally mine.*

He pulled her out from the enclosure and covered her right there on the floor, nudging her knees open with his. His stomach slid against hers, his abs nestling against her softness. His arms braced on either side of her head, the collar still clasped in one hand. He pressed into her with a slow, deliberate pace, watching the delight and arousal in her features. He slid out again and she urged him forward with her hips, and then they were moving together in a frantic joining.

"Were you dreaming of me, kitten? As you were told?"

"Yes, Master. Oh God!" She sighed as he drove his hips against her, into her tightness and warmth.

"Did it feel as good as this?"

"No...no...Master...this feels almost too good."

He chuckled. "Too good? Not too good for a little slavegirl who needs to come to please her Master. Twice at least."

She ended up coming three times, over and over, as he fought to keep her contained under him. She twisted and bucked, her eyes alive as she gazed at him. He finally climaxed too, a thunderous orgasm triggered by her third vociferous one. They came to rest in a tangle of arms and legs. He stared down at her, brushing her locks out of her face. He couldn't stop the smile that bloomed across his face.

"Okay, I believe you. You really do want my collar."

Molly beamed back at him. "I want it forever. Master." She added the *Master* when she remembered, but the *forever* was the word that echoed in his mind. Did he want this forever? It wasn't fair to collar her otherwise. He knew Molly loved until death. Until after death, he amended, remembering her playing her violin for Clayton the day before. The silence of the cemetery had carried all her sweet words to him, although he didn't intentionally eavesdrop.

"I love you, Molly," he said to her. "I always will." His fingers trembled a little on the clasp. Once he clicked the small lock into place, she wouldn't be able to get it off without his assistance. He fastened the collar around her neck, and that was that. Now, always. Forever. "It looks good on you," he said softly.

She didn't say anything, just touched the collar with a kind of reverence and then launched herself into his embrace.

* * * * *

"Molly girl. Either get it in gear and get dressed, or you'll be back on the trestle instead of having dinner. Our reservations are for seven. Sharp."

Molly looked over her shoulder in the mirror at her Master. He looked fine in everyday clothes, but when he dressed up he really looked...sinful. Sinfully hot. She was torn now between staring at her beautiful new collar and staring at him, when what she really needed to do was dry her hair and finish getting ready to go out.

But oh...so beautiful. Her new collar was so beautiful. She hadn't known what it would look like until he'd come striding into the room with it dangling from his fingertips. She couldn't stop touching it now, it was so pretty and shiny and sleek. It had an "M" on it for Master, which she loved most of all.

"Focus, Molly."

"Yes, Master."

Molly didn't need to go out, didn't need Mephisto to drop a lot of money on her to make this day special, but she knew he'd do it anyway, so she was determined to enjoy it and show him her appreciation. When she finally got done doing her hair, she dressed in a black cowl-neck sweater dress that framed her new collar perfectly. As a bonus, her black dress matched her Master's usual subdued garb. His suit jacket and slacks were black, set off by a crisp white shirt and a deep crimson tie. She hadn't seen Mephisto in a suit and tie since Clayton's funeral. This was really a big deal.

Well, she knew it was a big deal. They'd talked about their relationship and their future together for hours leading up to this day. In a way it was almost like vanilla people getting engaged. Not every slave collaring was that serious, but this one felt that way. Maybe she was just projecting her own desires into their conversations. Mephisto had never said anything specific about marriage in their future. If Master Mephisto wanted to marry her some day as her old Master had, she would be thrilled, but she wouldn't expect to have all those plans laid out for her just yet.

No, they needed time to adjust to this first. Love, slavery, connection. *I love you, Molly. I always will*, he'd said. But he might have just meant the love of a Master for a slave, or even the love of a mentor or protector for a protégé. The love of a friend. He'd been all those things to her. At the restaurant, she gazed into his eyes to find them shining with a deep intensity that made her stomach flip-flop.

"What are you thinking about?" he asked. "You're very thoughtful tonight."

Molly cast around for something to say besides *I'm thinking about whether you'll marry me*. "I was just remembering...I don't know. Our history together. All the things you've done for me, Mas—" She clamped her lips shut and fingered the silver chain around her neck. She wasn't supposed to call him Master in public. She took a sip of wine and looked down at the table, then back at him. "This almost feels like a culmination, in a way. Something we've been building toward for years."

He nodded. "It does feel that way, doesn't it? I've been trying to put that into words for days but you beat me to it."

"But at the same time...those old days when we first met...even that week you watched me for Clayton...they seem a lifetime ago. Or another life entirely."

Mephisto chuckled. "Sometimes they seem that way to me too." He sighed and lingered a moment over his Chicken Piccata. "The truth is, when you came to stay with me that week, I thought I knew you pretty well already, but I didn't know you at all. You surprised me in so many ways."

Molly laughed, leaning across the table to fix him with a look of mock reproach. "You surprised me too. You *traumatized* me."

"Did I? I would have thought you'd already expect the worst of me."

"I did, but your worst was worse than anything I could have dreamed."

He made an outraged face. "I wasn't that awful to you."

"You were awful," Molly insisted.

"Okay, I was pretty mean. It was a hard week for you. But you know, there was a purpose to my madness. I was testing you."

"Testing me for what?"

He paused. "For truth. I wanted to break you down and get some truth out of you, out of that slavey little shell you were in. I guess deep down I couldn't believe you were really happy, as hardcore as you were with Clayton. I worried about Stockholm Syndrome, mind control, all those things. I wanted to reassure myself that you really wanted the life you had with him."

It felt strange to hear these things now. Back then she'd only thought he wanted to torture her. He'd denied her speech, denied her pleasure, kept her locked in a chastity belt. He'd stored her in a cage, fucked other women—and men—in front of her. On the last day, he'd asked her questions that troubled her, and forced her to answer them, but she'd never known the answers he sought. She understood better now. "You know, I was so happy with him. But there were times I..." She looked away, unable to meet his gaze. *There were times I wanted other men too. Like you.*

She was thankful Mephisto didn't press her to finish her sentence. Instead, he said, "You've changed, you know. From the person you were then."

Molly nodded. "I know."

"It's like Clayton's passing forced you to find this inner strength you didn't know you had. I mean, I always knew you had it. I wasn't sure if you knew."

"So it was my inner strength that made me go crazy and trash Clayton's house, and party like a maniac?"

"No, that was your inner insanity," said Mephisto with a snort. "Let's hope that stays away from now on. No, I'm talking about the way you've stepped up to the plate with Clayton's family, Clayton's lawyers, handling his estate. You know, I talked to him about you on many occasions. I don't think he ever suspected you'd be strong enough to kick so much ass without him. I think he would have been pleasantly surprised to see you today."

Burn For You

Molly stifled a laugh. "I think he would have been horrified. He liked me mindless and servile."

"And you enjoyed being that for him," Mephisto said. "Don't act like you didn't."

Molly flushed because it was true.

"But I'm glad," he added, "that you're ready to be a little more kick-ass. I find your combination of service and badassness completely intoxicating. I could spend my whole life with someone like you and be perfectly happy."

Oh, now. That sounded pretty committed, Molly thought. But then, they'd been working toward this for so long.

Mephisto slid a hand across the table to grasp hers. "Everything worked out, didn't it, Molly? We're so lucky. How many people get as lucky as us?"

"Not many."

It had to be luck, didn't it? Molly felt like the luckiest woman on earth.

CHAPTER TWELVE
DETOUR

It was just a few weeks after that—around Thanksgiving—that Molly started developing health problems. Mephisto worried she was having some psychosomatic reaction to becoming his slave. She wouldn't eat, claiming a nervous stomach. She didn't want to sleep, but then she'd practically pass out from exhaustion when Mephisto ordered her to bed. He could tell from the drawn lines of her face she was dropping weight.

At first he thought she wasn't eating because she was worried about her figure. He knew Clayton used to measure her and weigh her obsessively. It was a pretty warped kink, but Mephisto had never noticed Molly suffering from any food or self-image issues. But now she was, and Mephisto examined his behavior to see if he was causing them. He fixed a variety of meals and ordered out food that she liked. He asked if she wanted more input into food preparation but she assured him she didn't, that she was fine. But she still didn't eat.

He didn't know how to deal with weight issues in slavery. Unlike Clayton, Mephisto wasn't comfortable micromanaging Molly's diet or controlling her intake of food. He didn't want to force her to eat, but her loss of appetite was alarming. Then the intermittent lethargy and nausea began.

To his frustration, Molly insisted she was okay, insisted on continuing to serve him even when she was swaying on her feet. This wasn't how he'd pictured things...his slave gagging miserably on his cock every time she sucked it, and turning green every time he tried to coax her to eat. She winced and almost retched as he held out a piece of toasted flatbread topped with feta.

"You love Greek, kitten." He sighed. "I went out and got this especially for you."

She fell to her knees and pressed her forehead against his calf. "Master, please punish me if I've displeased you."

"Punish you? Honey, something's wrong with you and I want to know what it is." He took her arm and made her lift her gaze to his. "I want you to make an appointment with a doctor."

"I'm fine, Master. This will pass, I'm sure. A doctor will make a fuss about the marks."

He studied the fading cane tracks on her thighs and frowned. "I won't make any more marks on you. When the existing ones are gone, I want you in for a full work up. A complete physical. What if this is something more serious than a stomach bug? Stomach bugs don't usually last three weeks."

"I'll go to the doctor, Master. If you wish it." She sounded like she wished for anything but.

Mephisto stroked her cheek and gave her a sympathetic look. "I know you hate doctors, but part of being a good Master is keeping my slave—you—in good health. You look...sickly."

She cringed. "I'm sorry, Master." For fuck's sake, like this illness was somehow her fault.

"Molly girl." He waited until she looked up at him. "You understand I'm not angry with you. I just want to find out what's going on. You've lost weight, and..." He thought a moment. When had she had her last period? He couldn't remember her having one since they'd started sleeping together again. "Do you usually miss periods?"

Burn For You

"I do sometimes, since Master had my tubes tied."

She took a tiny bite of the food he held out to her, struggling to choke it down. The girl would do anything to please him, and she'd done even more for Clayton, given up so much. Even her fertility. "I still can't believe Clayton made you do that," he said. "You were so young. Why did you agree to it?"

She shook her head. "Oh, no. I asked him to, Master. I begged him. I didn't want anything to take any of my attention away from him."

Mephisto snorted. "Like a baby? You don't know the meaning of play, you know. It's all or nothing with you."

She looked down at the floor. "I wanted to concentrate on his needs."

"Yes, well, that's enough on the subject." Her tone came awfully close to being disrespectful. He reached to stroke one of her breasts, but he noticed the subtle flinch.

Her breasts hurt. They were fuller, even though she was dropping weight. Some nagging idea starting knocking at the periphery of his brain. "Wait." He rubbed his forehead. "You asked Clayton to sterilize you?"

"Yes, Master. I had a miscarriage and I had to have surgery for it, and I guess while I was already under, they tied my tubes."

All the air in Mephisto's lungs whooshed out in a rush. "You *guess* they tied your tubes?" *Clayton. You fucker. Fucker. Fucker, fucker, fucker.* Clayton had been obsessed with making plans for his slave's future...for his slave's inevitable life after him. Would he have sterilized Molly in her early twenties? Would any doctor have agreed to do it?

"Did you sign anything?" Molly looked alarmed at the sudden anger in his voice, but Mephisto was slowly imploding. He wanted to smack himself in the head. How could he have been so stupid? "Did you sign anything? Answer me!"

She wrung her hands in her lap. "Sign what?"

"Some paper giving consent. A surgical release to have your tubes tied."

She shook her head. "My Master took care of all that."

Fucker. *Fucker.* Took care of it by getting a vasectomy, no doubt, and lying to Molly for the remaining duration of their marriage. Neither one of them had a clue about sane and consensual play. Clayton had let her believe she'd been sterilized and taken his own steps to prevent another baby. Fucker.

"You would have had to sign some paper at the hospital." His voice was breaking, because he *knew.* Molly shrank away from him. He shouldn't take his anger out on her, but it coiled and buzzed inside him, needing escape.

Clayton Copeland. Selfish, megalomaniacal prick. He'd lied to Mephisto's face, told him Molly was sterile. Why? Mephisto only had to ponder that for a moment. It was because Mephisto would have told her if he'd known the truth. He would have told her two years ago when she stayed with him. A woman should know if she was fertile or not, goddamn it. Apparently Molly wasn't the only one who didn't know how far to take power exchange play.

He looked down at the girl at his feet. Full breasts, darker nipples. Nausea and exhaustion. "Oh my God, Molly. They don't just tie a young woman's tubes without her express, written consent," he said. "Without some kind of counseling, for God's sake. It's just not done."

"My Master signed everything, I'm sure," Molly insisted. "He took care of everything."

"In your happy little imaginary kink world, yes. But there are procedures that have to be followed in the real world, in hospitals, in operating rooms. God!" He grabbed his head and laid it on the table, praying for calm.

"What's the matter?"

"What's the matter?" Mephisto echoed bitterly. "You're not sterile, my love. I don't think you are. Not at all."

"My Master said—"

"Your Master lied to you. Many times. Jesus. If you never signed anything—you, specifically—your tubes weren't tied, I promise you." He raised his head and looked at her, at her terrified gaze. "You aren't sick, Molly. You're pregnant."

Her mouth dropped open and her hand went to her waist. Now that he studied her, now that he scrutinized her changing body, he saw a thickening there, even though her face and arms were thinner. She shook her head, but that couldn't undo the reality of it. She was knocked up, pregnant, and judging from her lack of periods, three months gone at least. Nausea, exhaustion, loss of appetite... Mephisto had read stories of women going into labor who'd never realized they were pregnant. While entertaining, he'd always thought to himself, "No way." He'd never imagined such a thing was possible, but now he believed, because he knew Molly like his own heart, and had seen all the signs, and still he hadn't realized...

Hadn't realized she was pregnant with his child.

Her face was blank, shocked. Her bottom lip trembled until she bit down on it hard. Then she was up, running down the hall. He followed, only to have the bathroom door slammed in his face. He could hear her retching, then vomiting. Coughing. Sobbing. Mephisto understood the impulse, unfortunately. Not that he wanted to cry. No, he wanted to rage. He wanted to go trample every flower on Clayton's grave and rail at his fancy fucking headstone. How dare he? How dare he do this to the both of them?

Mephisto had a feeling Clayton had wanted this to happen all along. He felt topped from beyond the grave. He opened the door intending to help his slave, only to have her scoot out and run from him again, heading for the bedroom.

"Do not," Mephisto thundered. "Do not get in that goddamn cage."

She froze and spun to face him. She was actually cowering, and it angered Mephisto even more.

"Don't look like that," he yelled. "Like you did something wrong. Like you deserve to be punished for this."

She backed away, hugging herself. "But you're angry."

"I'm not angry at you, damn it. I'm angry at your old Master, that son of a bitch. That fucking prick."

"Please...Master..." Her voice quavered and she hugged herself tighter, then she seemed to realize she was cradling her waist, and dropped her hands to her sides.

"Oh, Molly," he sighed. "Come here."

She came into his outstretched arms, but she held herself stiffly. He ran his hands over her back, over her shaking shoulders, trying to comfort her and gain control of himself. She didn't deserve his fury— and she didn't need to be coping with it now on top of everything else.

"I should have known. I should have questioned sooner," he said. "But at least we know what's wrong with you now. At least we know it's nothing serious. Well..." He shook his head, correcting himself. "It's serious, but not fatal. It's not cancer or kidney failure or something like that."

"Maybe I'm not pregnant." Her voice sounded small and scared. "I don't feel pregnant. I think I'm probably not pregnant."

Mephisto stared down at her breasts, at her little stomach pressing against him. *God, Molly. A child. Yours and mine.* He was horrified and excited at the same time.

"I think I'm probably not pregnant. I think it's a stomach virus." She caught his gaze, frowned at the conflicted smile playing at the corners of his lips.

"Molly, you're pregnant."

"I might not be."

"If you're not, I'll get down on my knees and serve you instead. I'll let you put me into chastity as long as you like. Cage me. The whole deal."

She looked traumatized. "I don't want to do that, Master!"

"Good, because you won't get the chance. You're pregnant."

When she would have protested again, he put a finger to her lips.

"We can find out in about fifteen minutes. We're going to pick up a pregnancy test, right now." He oriented her toward the closet and gave her a little nudge. "Get dressed."

* * * * *

153

Going to the pharmacy to purchase the pregnancy test was one of the most gut-wrenching experiences of Molly's life. She didn't even have to do anything, just trail along at her Master's side while he selected the test and took it to the counter to pay for it, but it was still so difficult. She had to force one foot in front of the other. She had to appear composed and not start crying in a panic, because people would get upset. Her Master would get upset, and his anger earlier had scared her enough.

The cashier was a bored college guy on the evening shift. As he rang up their single item, he shot a look at her that was embarrassingly sympathetic. No one else seemed to notice what was going on. Two tween girls giggled by the lipstick testers. A mother scolded her child, refusing to buy him candy. Molly stood and watched banal reality from her own sideways world.

Her old Master had lied to her. Not a small, kinky lie. A big, serious lie. A lie that kind of devastated her. A lie that broke her heart.

I'm sure he did it for you, Master Mephisto told her as she'd cried in the car. *He knew you would have wanted to be the one sterilized for him.* It was true. She would have felt terrible if she'd known her Master underwent a vasectomy for her, all because she didn't want to risk another baby. She would have felt selfish and awful. It was bad enough to ask him to have her tubes tied. But the miscarriage had been so bloody, so scary. So painful. There had been an infection. Incomplete miscarriage. She couldn't do anything right, even miscarry a baby. And now this.

Her Master was pretending to be calm about it, but she'd seen his anger. His regret. He didn't want a baby. *But you want one*, her subconscious whispered. *One that survives this time, with a man you love.*

Back at the club, in the back where she and her Master lived, Molly hovered over the toilet, pissing on a plastic stick while Mephisto stared at her. Just like at the pharmacy, reality continued unabated around them. His employees were starting to arrive outside. Club patrons would be coming soon. Instead of greeting them, he was holding the stick she'd handed him. He watched it for about fifteen seconds, then set it on the counter and wordlessly gave her the other one from the box.

She peed again, miserably. She couldn't pee as much this time, but the stick was mostly wet. She wondered if tears would work to fill out the rest of the absorbent tip. She handed it to him, thinking wildly for a moment of holding two pregnancy tests to her eyes, soaking the thick white wicks with hysterical crying. That resulted in a maniacal giggle she had to choke back. Mephisto glanced up from the second test.

"You okay, kitten?"

No, I'm not okay at all. That's a definite 'no' for that question.

"Can you get off there?" he said. "I don't want to tell you the results while you're perched on a toilet."

Molly wiped and stood up, then backed toward the counter as he approached with the two tests between his fingers. He held them out to her, under the harsh light of the vanity. "Two lines is pregnant. Both these tests have two lines. Two dark lines." Molly swallowed hard as her Master stroked her cheek. "Little slavegirl, you're definitely pregnant."

Of course she was. She'd known she was as soon as he'd said it in the kitchen. But there was still the possibility of denial before the test. Now, no more denial. She looked up at him through tears.

"What are we going to do?"

He set the tests on the counter beside her and sighed. "What do you want to do?"

Molly wanted him to fix this. That's what she wanted. She wanted him to tell her what to do, but she knew he wouldn't. His dark brown eyes burned into hers. "I'm not sure what you're asking me, Master."

"I'm asking you whether you want to keep it or not, of course. I have my own opinion on the matter, but I'd like to hear yours first."

His mouth and lips were tight, like he was holding his own opinion back. She tried to read his expression, but he was being carefully impassive. "Master, I— Do you—"

He held up a hand. "No. I don't want you to do what I want. You aren't getting any orders from me, not now, not about this. What do you want to do? This is the second time I'm asking. I'll give you time to think if you like, but don't look to me for your answer."

"I—I d-don't need time to think. I want to have it. I'm sorry if you don't want to, Master. If you don't want to—"

His lips twitched. "If I don't want to, then what? Will you choose my will over that life inside you?"

Hot tears spilled over her cheeks. If he didn't want it, then what? How could she find such a wonderful Master and lose him so soon? It wasn't like she wouldn't be okay. She had money, a safe place to stay. She knew she would love this baby. But to be without her Master—

He took her face in his hands. "What are you crying about, kitten? You don't have to choose. Of course I want this baby, but I want you to want it too."

A pent up breath of panic left her in a whoosh. He hugged her close and kissed her, then wiped away her tears. "No, no...no more crying. Not now. This is happy. You'll be a great mother. I always thought so. I always thought it was a shame, what Clayton did...but actually didn't do."

Memory crashed down on her. Her hands flew to her middle.

"I lost the last one," she cried. "At eleven weeks. Maybe I'll lose this one too. Maybe something's wrong with me."

"I think the only thing wrong with you is that you have way too many unfounded worries. Let's get you an appointment with an OB and see what's going on. How far along you are, how the baby looks. Or babies. Maybe it's twins."

Molly almost vomited. Twins?

They waited a week to visit the obstetrician. It took that long to get an appointment with the kink-friendly one Mephisto knew, but Molly and Mephisto both agreed it had to be someone who would understand their dynamic. Molly didn't think she could go through a whole pregnancy without any marks, at the very least some light bruises. Mephisto also pointed out that a kink-friendly doctor would know what activities they could safely continue to do and which ones they'd have to give up for the time being.

At the appointment, Dr. Willetts eyed Molly's collar briefly as he talked to her about her symptoms and her previous miscarriage. It felt nice not to have to hide their dynamic, or pretend the collar was just a necklace with a charm.

It probably also made more sense when they told the doctor about the ordeal of Molly's tubes being tied...but not really. He did raise his eyebrows a bit when he heard the whole tale. The doctor faxed over an order to the hospital where she'd had her surgery and found no notes in Molly's records about her tubes being tied. "So, my dear," he said in an ironic tone, "going forward, please remember you are one hundred percent fertile."

After they talked, Dr. Willetts did an ultrasound to see how far along she was. Thirteen to fourteen weeks, give or take. Molly gawked at the shapeless little blob as he measured the skull, the arms and legs. A little butterfly fluttered in its chest. A strong, steady heartbeat.

"You've already got a trimester under your belt," Dr. Willetts said. "And I know you'll worry because of your last pregnancy, but based on your blood work and what I can see in this ultrasound, everything's good. Your last pregnancy likely ended a few weeks before the miscarriage even started, so to be at fourteen weeks now with a healthy baby...this is a good thing."

Molly nodded but worry still curled in her chest. It had been terrible to lose Clayton's baby. She wasn't sure she could go through it again. She hadn't even gotten a chance to see that baby on ultrasound, to see the rapidly beating heart, the tiny limbs that moved and floated inside her.

"Holy God," Mephisto breathed. "That's a baby."

Mephisto saw a baby, but Molly saw something more. *Their* baby.

Mephisto whistled under his breath. "Fourteen weeks." He eyed Molly's waistline. "I'm surprised you're not showing more by now, kitten."

The doctor looked unconcerned. "She'll begin to show soon. Really show. With petite women, a first pregnancy especially, they don't show at first, and then bam, they look huge."

Molly wasn't too thrilled about the whole *bam, they look huge* idea. Mephisto grinned at her. "So," he said, turning to the doctor. "If she's at fourteen weeks, can you tell us the date it was conceived? Approximately?"

"Sure." The doctor pointed to a date on the ultrasound screen. "It would have been around the end of August. The baby should arrive sometime around mid-May."

Molly and Mephisto's eyes locked across the room. May 16th was her former Master's birthday.

Suddenly, eerily, it felt like there were four—no, five—of them in the room.

CHAPTER THIRTEEN
YES MASTER

Mephisto entered Lorna's BDSM shop and sauntered around for a while before she stuck her head out from the back. She came to greet him, one eyebrow raised, lips pursed.

"Master Mephisto, I've been waiting for you to come see me. But I'm afraid it's a little late for a chastity belt to work."

Mephisto laughed. "I didn't come in for a chastity belt." He leaned against a display of glass dildos and quirked a smile at her. "I see you heard the news."

"Only from every customer who's been by in the last month."

"And..."

Lorna cocked her head thoughtfully. "How did it happen? You can't have been trying. Now that I think about it, didn't Clayton spay her? I seem to remember that being a topic of gossip at some point."

"Spay her? She's a slave, not a cat."

Lorna sniffed. "Don't you call her 'kitten?'"

Mephisto sighed. "No, he didn't 'spay' her, but she thought he did. So did I. Long story." He waved his hand. "Anyway, I need your help. You have three kids, don't you?"

"Yes, I do, my friend." She put down the paperwork she was looking at to focus on him. "Pushed all three out of my vagina after excruciating and torturous labors. Why?"

"Molly's a little nervous about childbirth. I thought maybe you could give me some advice. You know, things to say to reassure her."

"Aw, that's cute. Man doesn't know how to cope with his woman's mysterious natural functions. Has to call in a female friend for backup. Very sweet."

"I'm serious. I don't know anything about labor or birth, or babies for that matter."

"So take a class like everyone else. My three are all grown up now. I hardly remember giving birth." She blew her breath out. "Thank God for that."

Mephisto watched his friend busy herself with another task. If he didn't know better— "Lorna, are you angry with me about something?"

She gave a sharp laugh, then put down the vibrators she was tinkering with. "Okay, yes. I'm a little upset. What's going on here? What are you doing? Clayton's barely a year in his grave."

"She's my slave now. She's collared. We're committed to each other."

"And now you're having a baby? Molly's a baby herself."

"She's not," Mephisto cut in. "Not anymore."

"Women like Molly never grow up. What kind of mother will she be?"

"She's changed in the last year. She's not the same person she was."

"You'll end up raising the child yourself, mark my words. You'll be parenting both of them. As for your precious dynamic, your collar and your mastery of her, you can kiss that goodbye from here on out."

Lorna looked bitter, and yes, angry. "It's not going to work that way with us," he said. "So I guess that's a 'no' on having a chat with her?"

"You know—" Lorna stopped, collected herself. "For a lot of us here, you've always been the one who had his shit together, the one in charge. You've always been the center of the Seattle kink universe, but now we all feel like we're losing you. To her."

"To Molly. You can say her name. It's not cursed."

"Fine. We all feel like we're losing you to Molly. It's not a good feeling."

Mephisto thought a moment, choosing his words carefully. "I can see how it feels that way, but you're not losing me to anyone. I'm changing, just as she's changed. If you're my friend, if you care about me, you have to accept that and let it happen. And you have to stop panicking and assuming this is somehow the beginning of the end. It's not the beginning of the end, it's just the beginning of something different. It will take a lot more than me and Molly pairing up to kill the Seattle kink scene."

He strolled over to Lorna—carefully. She was a judo expert. When he didn't get a roundhouse kick to the neck, he felt confident enough to take her hand. "Can I hug you, Mistress?" he asked.

"Sure. If you don't mind getting your nuts surgically removed from your gall bladder after I knee them up there."

He hugged her anyway, until her tight leather corset creaked beneath his strong embrace. "You don't have to talk to Molly. You don't even have to like her, even though it saddens me, since you're my closest friend. You don't have to be happy for us. But please—don't worry. Nothing is ending. I'm not going anywhere, I'm not going vanilla, and I sure as hell am not giving up my stranglehold over all the pervs of Seattle. I'm too controlling to do that."

"You are controlling," Lorna conceded gruffly.

"But if I do go vanilla, I give you permission to hunt me down and domme me into submission until I rediscover myself."

"Can I nail your cock to a two-by-four?"

"Um..."

"Will this be a no-limits type of arrangement? I could get into that."

"Limits will be my cock, nails, and two-by-fours."

She pushed him away. "Already getting so tame." Then she smiled in spite of herself and crossed her arms over her chest. "You know, you'll make a great dad. Even if I find the whole idea disgusting."

"Hey, I find the idea of you having three kids kind of disgusting too, considering your predilection for nailing cocks to wood."

"Only your cock, Mephisto. Only the best cock earns the nails."

He shuddered and took a step away from her. "I'm glad we had this talk. I'd actually like you to stay the hell away from Molly at this point, if you don't mind."

They both laughed then. When they sobered, things felt peaceful again, copacetic between them. "I respect you so much, Lorna. If you ever change your mind, I think you and Molly could find more common ground for friendship than you think."

Lorna didn't answer, only turned her attention away from him. Mephisto walked out. He knew by now when he was dismissed.

* * * * *

Molly made a beautiful pregnant woman. Before sex, before play, Mephisto would make her walk around and flaunt her belly and breasts for him. Pure porn. Not that he wouldn't enjoy having his wispy slavegirl back at some point, but for now he was enjoying watching her bloom. Over the past four months, the guest room had been turned into a nursery outfitted in sage and cream. Gender neutral. Their baby had been persistently coy in revealing its sex during ultrasounds. Mephisto was strongly opposed to pink and blue indoctrination anyway. Sage and cream suited him just fine.

And their sex life? Lorna had been off, way off. They were hornier and kinkier than ever. Mephisto's imagination exploded with twisted pregnancy fantasies. He liked to pretend she was his breeding slave, that she was bearing child after child for his pleasure. Sometimes they played Christian Fundamentalists and had awkward, tender sex in the missionary position around her big belly while they prayed about the sanctity of life. His favorite by far, though, was the forced-pregnancy fantasy.

"Come here, kitten," he said, gesturing to her. She crossed the room, snuggling into his arms. He ran a finger down her cheek, his other hand caressing her rounded tummy. "I want to play the thing where I'm impregnating you against your will. Again."

Molly giggled, looking down at her 7-month waistline. "It's getting harder and harder to buy into the 'I'm gonna knock you up, bitch' thing. When I'm so obviously...you know...knocked up already."

He put a finger over her lips. "Silence, naughty slavegirl. The correct answer is 'Yes, Master, I'd be delighted to act out that fantasy for you.'"

Molly laughed some more while he went to the bed and started arranging pillows and some sex cushions he'd ordered through Lorna's shop. "All we have to do," he explained patiently, "is fix it so the belly doesn't show."

When the pillows and cushions were propped just right, he beckoned her over.

"Would you like me to fight you, Master?" she asked.

He rolled his eyes. "I should beat you just for asking that question."

Ah, nothing like a struggling, pleading slave. He appreciated the way she threw herself into the acting, pulling away from him, screaming and crying. It was a Monday night. The club was empty; otherwise his dungeon masters and bouncers would have come running at her panicked screams. He put a hand over her mouth.

"Scream all you want...Mary Louise. You're having a baby for me whether you want to or not."

She choked on a laugh and broke out of her role. "Mary Louise?"

He gave her a sharp slap to her flank. "Good slaves don't laugh at their Masters. Now you'll have to be impregnated *and* punished."

Ha, he would have punished her anyway and she knew it. She gave a little shiver and launched back into character, dragging her heels and pushing at him as he practically carried her to the bed. He forced her forward onto his nest of cushioning.

"Okay?" he whispered. "You have enough support?"

"Yes, Master."

He held her down while he groped for the cuffs that were permanently affixed to their bed frame. He restrained her wrists first, then slid down the bed to capture her kicking feet. She came really close to taking out his cock with one kick. It was a big target—he was hugely hard. "You're a bad, bad girl," he yelled, slapping each of her flexing ass cheeks when he finally had her tied down. She was more or less on her knees, bent forward, the cushions cradling her belly. Oh yes, her ass was his.

"Let me go," she screamed, struggling against her bonds. "I don't want a baby."

"I didn't ask you, did I?" he yelled back.

"Let me go, you asshole. When I get away from you, I'm calling the police. You're going to be so fucked."

"No," he said, leaning down to stare in her eyes. "*You're* fucked. Because you're never getting away from me. I'm going to put my baby in you and you'll be tied to me for life. You'll stay with me and my baby and we'll be one big happy family, or else it will be the bad-girl cage for you. Do you understand?"

Molly spit at him. Jesus Christ, she was getting good at this roleplaying stuff. "Never. Never, never, *never*," she screamed.

He grabbed a handful of her hair. "You're going to regret that, my little spitfire. Bad girls get punished until they learn to be good." He went over to the closet and picked up one of his thick leather belts. He doubled it over and held it in front of her face. It spoke a lot to her trust of him, that even now, heavily pregnant, she'd let him play with her like this. She knew he would be carefully controlled. God, he would never harm her. Hurt her though? Yes, he was about to hurt her a lot.

He landed a sharp crack on her left cheek. His cock bucked as she squirmed. He smacked the right cheek next, then both in a resounding *whap*. She wailed in protest, not as Molly, but as his unwilling captive. "Stop it! Stop hitting me."

"When you've learned your lesson," he said with a hard voice.

Whap, whap, whap. He wasn't hitting her full force, but he was hitting her enough to excite her sexually. Her pussy was already glistening wet.

"Stop. Please!" she said after several more stingers.

"I'll stop when I believe you've been punished enough, and then I'll plant my baby in you."

"No!"

He gave her a really hard stroke then. She cried out and started sobbing. It was possibly real.

"I don't want a baby. Please let me go. Please, I'll do anything."

He flung the belt aside and went back to look at her face. "I don't want *anything*. Don't you get that by now? There's only one thing I want."

"You can fuck me," she pleaded. "Mouth, ass, even my pussy, as long as you wear a condom. If you come inside me, I'll get pregnant and I don't want to."

He looked down his nose at her. "You don't have a choice. Not anymore."

He knelt behind her on the bed. No way could he hold out any longer, and Molly was looking pretty sexed up too. She was grinding her hips against the cushions, arching her back. "No," she wailed, even as she opened her legs a little wider. He shoved the head of his cock against her pussy and then eased in. She twisted, pretending to fight him, and oh God, it felt so good he almost came off inside her right then.

Molly gasped as he entered her. "No, no," she yelled, but her pussy was screaming, *oh yes!* Her clit had started buzzing as soon as she started fighting him, and now, tied up and fucked, her whole body was on fire. "No, I don't want your baby."

Mephisto pounded her harder, grasping her aching ass cheeks. "You're not leaving this bed until you've got a load of my cum in your uterus. Maybe two loads. I can't wait to see you get big and round with my baby."

Molly buried her head in the pillows to stop herself from laughing. The stuff he came out with in the middle of these scenes... "I don't want your cum in my uterus," she yelled once she composed herself, and then it was him chuckling behind her. Oh God, the way his cock stretched her, hitting her right at her g-spot. "Please...please." He slowed, grinding on her. She clenched the sheets in her hands and held her breath. "Oh...oh, oh!"

"You want to come, don't you?" Mephisto's deep, raspy voice only made her burn hotter. "But if you come, it's going to make me come. As soon as your pussy clamps down on me..."

Oh, God, oh God!

"As soon as you come, it's going to milk the baby juice right out of me."

Molly dissolved into more helpless laughter. Baby juice? "I want to come," she whined. "I have to come."

"Come for me, baby. Come on." His voice was gruff and urgent. She sucked in a breath and let it out, her whole body vibrating with a need for release. "Oh, please, Master," she whispered. He slowed, fucking her deep, in and out. His balls slapped against her clit. She tensed her hips and felt herself open and catch fire. She made some kind of animal noise, thinking of nothing but his cock driving into her and wringing her out. Her climax rolled wide and nothing mattered for long seconds but the pleasure, the ecstasy soaking her like a rain shower. He was the storm, pounding into her, driving her down.

His arms braced beside her, hard muscles clenching, as he let out his breath beside her ear. "You're a good girl," he whispered. "My beautiful good girl."

When Molly caught her breath, she whispered, "Do you want to do the cage part now?"

"Oh, yes," he sighed. He undid her cuffs and helped her up and over to the cage. She felt awkward now climbing in and out but she still fit, even seven months pregnant. He reached in to caress her belly.

"See, this works perfectly for this part now."

"Yes, Master."

"Okay, rest a little bit. I'll bring you some water."

"Okay. Thank you, Master."

After she had some water, she drowsed, surrounded by pillows and soft feather blankets. She wasn't sure how long it was, but then her Master was back, tapping at her cage. He stared in at her, at her nakedness, the mound of her waistline. She pitched her voice to a begging whine.

"Please, I'm hungry."

"My baby makes you hungry, doesn't it?"

She nodded, feigning misery. "Please may I eat something? I'm really, really craving ice cream."

"You'll get spinach."

"Oh, please," she wailed. "I hate spinach."

"Spinach is good for the baby."

"Please. You don't understand how strong these food cravings are."

"There's a way to get ice cream. You know what it is, don't you?"

Her eyes filled with tears. She loved playing this part. "You know I don't like that. I'm already having a damn baby for you against my will. Why do you make me do that too?"

He shrugged. "If you want the ice cream..." He watched her another couple moments. "Okay, I'll go get the spinach."

"No!" She shuddered. "Okay, I'll do it."

Mephisto's eyes darkened. "Then I'll get the lube. Come on out. On your hands and knees. Get ready for me."

Oh, hell. She was ready all right. She loved anal, even though Mephisto was more gentle on her the more pregnant she got. She couldn't wait until a few months from now when he got back to the serious ass-raping, but for now, she was enjoying the dubious consent play. She moaned softly as he returned and knelt behind her. "Please, I don't want to. Can't I give you a blowjob for the ice cream?"

"Sure," he said. "You can do that too."

He stood and came around the front of her, yanked her head up and gave her a nice, firm facefucking for a minute or two. Molly drifted, feeling hot and used and taken advantage of in the most sexy of ways. "Please!" she said when he let her come up for air.

"Please fuck your ass? I'd be happy to." She braced on her arms as he went behind her. This position was actually really relaxing for her back. He smeared a dab of cool lube across her anus and then his thick cock pressed into her. She felt discomfort, then pain, then the welcome release as her body capitulated to the intrusion and let him in. She almost collapsed. She felt so full, so vulnerable and controlled by him.

"Oh, God, it hurts," she sighed, and it did hurt a little. It always hurt, which is why she loved it so much. Even when the sharp pain eased, there was still the discomfort. The knowledge that yes, he was hurting and invading her to take his pleasure. Ahh, her clit throbbed hard as she pondered that. It felt so good she almost forgot they were roleplaying. She finally yelled out some words to keep the fantasy going. "You're hurting me. I hate you for doing this to me! For making me have your baby. For making me have anal sex and making me...eat...spinach!"

He tightened his grip on her hips. "Just close your eyes and think of ice cream."

"Your cock is hurting my ass."

He drove a little deeper, a little harder. "How about now? Still hurt?"

"Ohhh..." Her breath sighed out and she sucked it in again. She wouldn't be able to keep up the acting much longer, because her brain was quickly emptying of blood. It was collecting instead in her nipples, in her pussy. She bucked back against him, driven on by his grunts and his rough grasp at her waist and hips. He slid his hand down and clasped her center, one finger swirling to circle her swollen clit.

"Ah, see," he sighed. "That feels better now, doesn't it?"

"Yes. Yes, it feels wonderful."

"You lied to me, little girl. You love having your ass fucked. I think I should still make you eat the spinach."

"No!"

"Yes. For lying to me. Although if you come hard enough, I might soften my stance on that."

"I'll come for you. I'll come for you, just, please..."

Her hips jerked at each wicked tap and tease of her clit as his cock continued to pound her ass. "Now," he whispered. "Now, come for me. Now, now, now."

He thrust into her and stayed still, rocking against her, and then it was happening, exactly what he'd asked of her. She clenched around his cock, feeling pleasure suffuse her whole body. He fucked her a couple minutes more, spreading her ass cheeks, saying nasty, yummy things to her that brought on another small orgasm to carry her through his huge, rough one. Molly collapsed on her side, her middle still tingling with aftershocks of arousal.

"Jesus, Molly," her Master said. "I think you earned some ice cream. Any kind you want."

Molly smiled. She knew exactly what kind of ice cream she wanted. He did too.

* * * * *

Molly was coming to think of this as their park bench. Every time they came to this park and ate ice cream, they sat here. They'd sat here years ago, and in the months after Clayton's death, and now they sat here again.

"I love this kind of ice cream," Molly said. "I don't know why. It's kind of bland." She took another lick of her soft vanilla cone. "I think it's the consistency."

"You could get chocolate, you know. Swirl. You're more of a swirl girl, aren't you?"

She smiled at her Master. "Am I?" She kicked at the grass under the bench and pulled her coat more tightly around her. There was something she wanted to talk about with him, but it was uncomfortable to bring it up. "Master?"

"Yes, baby?"

"I worry sometimes that I'm not going to be a good mother. That I'm not fit to be a mother."

He frowned. "Not fit to be a mother? Are you kidding me?" He rubbed his forehead. "Okay, tell me why you feel that way."

"I don't know. I guess because I'm not like other people. Our kid will have a weird mom."

"You're not weird." He stopped, thought a moment. "Okay, you're weird, but I happen to think weird people make the best parents."

"Even...kinky parents? We have a cage under our bed, for God's sake. Our child's going to grow up in a BDSM club."

Mephisto chuckled. "I think before the baby gets too old we'll have to find another place. Maybe rent the back space out to an employee. But we'll handle it. So we're kinky, so what? It will just make the parent-teacher conferences a lot more interesting."

Molly looked around the park, at all the normal moms. She'd never count herself in that group, she knew that. She tried to be okay with it, but somewhere deep inside, she wanted to be normal, like them, with nothing to hide.

"Even now," he said softly. "You're still ashamed of who you are, aren't you?"

She didn't bother to deny it. "I'm sorry, Master."

"You don't have to be sorry. I wish I understood though. Yeah, kinky people are different. We're not your average Joe and Jane, but I'm not going to hang my head about it. Nothing we do is illegal or even immoral in my mind. Just because you and I are kinky doesn't mean we don't deserve to be parents, that we can't raise children as well as anyone else. And you have a legacy to pass on. Clayton's good works, and your good works now. You have a lot of money and influence that will need to be passed down one day to someone with a similar mindset on kindness and generosity. This is our chance to create that someone. Why shouldn't we, Molly? Why shouldn't we raise up a really wonderful human being?"

"Well, I want to do that. I'm just worried that since I'm not exactly normal, our kid won't turn out normal either."

"If we love him and nurture him, he'll turn out wonderful whether he's normal or not."

Molly looked over at him, surprised. "You said 'him.' Do you think it will be a boy?"

Mephisto shrugged. "I kind of do. I don't know why. Just a feeling. And I have a fifty percent chance of being right," he added with a laugh. "Listen, kitten. Don't worry. You'll be a great mom, and I'm going to bust my ass to be Dad of the Century. As for the rest, we'll be ourselves, to a point. We'll find more private ways of doing our kinky things. Sell the cage bed, move the other cage into a dark closet somewhere." He eyed her with a grin. "You got turned on a little just now, didn't you?"

Molly licked a long, teasing line along the length of her cone. "Yes, I did."

"Maybe we should start looking for an appropriately dark closet later when we get home."

"Oh yes, Master. And to be honest, I won't be sad to see the bad-girl cage go."

"Liar. You love that cage."

She smirked at him, suggestively assaulting her ice cream.

"Be careful, kitten," he muttered. "There are laws against public indecency, and if you push me too far, I'll break them all."

She studied him. He did look pretty keyed up, but then, he'd seemed that way since they'd gotten to the park. "Is everything okay, Master?" she asked. "I'm always leaning on you for my problems, but you never tell me any of yours."

He gave her a piercing, tender look that made her heart thump hard for a moment. "I don't have a whole lot of problems. When I do, you always make me feel better."

Molly ate the last of her cone and went into his arms. He held her close, pressing a kiss against her forehead. He held her so much these days, her belly didn't even feel awkward anymore jammed between them. Now and again the baby would kick and turn over—maybe a form of protest at being squeezed so much. She clung to him. "I love you, Master. I love you so much."

He didn't respond for a moment, although she felt a subtle change of tension in his body. "It was about three years ago, now. Since we sat here that first time. I think that was the first time I admitted to myself...God...'I really want her.' Now here you are."

She knew exactly what he was talking about. She sat up and smiled at him. "Three years. It's hard to believe. But then, not hard at all. So much has happened since then. So much has changed."

"Some things have changed. Other things have stayed the same." He looked away from her, across the park, his lips tightening. "All I could think about that day was how jealous I was of Clayton. That week, I wondered so many times what it would be like to be your Master, to own you and enjoy you whenever, however I liked."

He took her hand. Molly looked down at their interlaced fingers. "Well, you have that now. Is it everything you hoped?"

"Oh, Molly." He gazed into her eyes, then away again. "God, baby, it's so much more than I hoped. So much more fulfilling. So much deeper. I wanted your intelligence, your impeccable service. Your willpower. I never even understood about all the rest. The love, the closeness." He ran his thumb across her wrist, looking down at their hands. "Listen, it's time to say this. I think we should get married. I'd like to get married before our child is born. Even without a baby, I would have wanted to be with you forever. But with him...or her...on the way, we might as well make it official. What do you say?"

She couldn't say anything. Her heart was suddenly wedged tightly in her throat.

"I'm asking Molly, by the way. Not my kitten. Not my slavegirl. I'm asking you, and you can say yes or no, just like a vanilla woman."

Like a normal woman. Her lips curved in an irrepressible smile. "It's so normal, to get married. Maybe there's hope for us after all."

Mephisto snorted. "Well, I wouldn't go that far. Normal? I don't have a ring for you, except for this one," he said, touching the small ring that held her "M" charm. "I'll get you one after the baby comes. When you're not so..."

"Fat? Bloated?" Molly provided.

"Fluffy," he said, rubbing her perpetually swollen fingers. "You can help me pick it out."

"Thank you, Master. I think that sounds wonderful."

"So is that a yes? A yes from Molly, not a *Yes, Master, I'll do whatever you ask*?"

"Yes, Master. It's a yes from Molly." She looked up at the sky for a moment. "You're making me feel a little schizophrenic. But either way, the answer is yes."

He scrutinized her, a curl of amusement at the corner of his lips. "You know, I thought you'd be crying. I expected drama and waterworks. I'm a little disappointed."

Molly couldn't look away from those lips, that lovely smile. God, how she loved this man. "I can't cry. I'm too happy. And for once in my life, I'm not conflicted. This just seems so perfect and...right. Too perfect to cry over. Although..." She pulled out the most guilty-slave look from her arsenal and pasted it on her face. "If you're very disappointed, Master, I suppose you should punish me."

He rolled his eyes. "Toppy little slavegirl. This is what happens as soon as you pop the question. Sheesh."

"I'll never top you, I promise," Molly said, squeezing his fingers. "You can put it in the vows."

"Oh, our vows are going to be something special. I'm going to start writing them tonight. There might be something in there about a chastity belt."

Molly laughed and snuggled closer in his arms. "I hereby plight you my orgasms."

"Yes! I like the sound of that." Mephisto sighed. "I like the sound of that very much."

CHAPTER FOURTEEN
HAPPY

A wedding. Mephisto wouldn't have believed it, not even a year ago. Now he was standing in the middle of a motley group of kinky friends and well wishers in a city park, gazing into the eyes of the woman who meant the world to him.

He wasn't in a tux, although he'd worn his best black dress shirt and removed the chains that normally swung from this particular pair of jeans. And Molly wasn't in white, but in light blue with white flowers. It suited her. No frilly, billowing skirt, but a form fitting silk dress that outlined her beautiful pregnant curves. Her very pregnant curves.

They'd thrown it together quickly. They were on a deadline, after all—Molly's belly wasn't getting any smaller. Still, the wedding was exactly what he would have wanted it to be, even with years of planning. Intimate, emotionally moving. Best of all, they were among close friends. They'd asked Lorna to officiate, since when a Master married his slave, it was best to have a kinky person standing there overseeing the vows. Mistress Lorna looked striking in a black corset and fitted black pants. She intoned their vows in a deep, formal voice, looking at them over the edge of her cat-eye glasses.

"For richer, for poorer, in sickness and in health—"

"In handcuffs and in chains," a voice suggested from the back of the group. Laughter broke out as Lorna glared at the culprit.

"Let's respect the sanctity of this moment"—she arched one threatening brow—"or *I'll* be breaking out the handcuffs and chains, and you won't like it."

The ceremony concluded with no further outbursts, although Mephisto and Molly exchanged quite a few soft chuckles at Mistress Lorna's additions and ad-libs. As long as they were legally married, Mephisto didn't care what else they swore to each other. Whips, chains, chastity belts? It was all good.

They descended afterward on the club, to eat, drink, and watch everyone else play in a bacchanalian celebration of their union. They played a little too, with great caution. As it turned out, it was the last real play they did. Molly moved into her eighth month shortly afterward. Their appointments came more frequently. The doctor warned them to dial back the intensity of any scenes they did, but Mephisto was so afraid of harming her or the baby that he called a hiatus on play altogether until after the birth.

They still hung out in the club. In a way, watching and admiring the pleasure of others became a way for them to remain sexually close, even into her ninth month. The people they watched didn't mind, and he and Molly got to share in their ecstasy—and collect ideas. He would have liked to play with Molly, sure, but she could barely move, much less submit to a crop or flogger. He rubbed her lower back as she perched beside him near the spanking bench. A very noisy, very arousing scene was unfolding between a slick young dom and his lithe submissive— exhibitionists both.

Mephisto nudged her with a shoulder as they drank in the interaction. "Do you miss it?"

Molly tilted her head to the side, watching the sub's sinuous struggles. "You mean the spanking? Or having a waistline like that?"

Mephisto laughed and took her hand. "Oh, you'll get your waist back, kitten. I think you miss the playing more."

"God, yes, Master." She sighed in resignation. "I'd give anything just to wear a pair of nipple clamps right now."

He pitched his voice low and leaned close to speak in her ear. "I'll give you all the nipple clamps you want, very soon, girl. All you can bear," he added, arching one eyebrow.

She squeezed his hand, giving a little shudder. "Don't tease me, please, Master. That's just cruel."

He gave her a fortifying smile. "You love cruelty, my little maso. Don't worry, it won't be long now before we can get back to it."

"Mm," said Molly. "I thought the doctor said we had to wait at least six weeks."

"Six weeks is nothing. I lusted after you for years, Molly. I can do six weeks."

Poor Molly, sitting everything out. It meant he sat out too, even though she'd mustered up the courage last week to suggest he take on a temporary slave until she could serve him again. He'd slapped her on the ass and locked her in the cage until she felt better. She was otherwise doing pretty well. She was ready for childbirth, cocky about it even. "I love pain," she'd told him. "Labor will be nothing to me."

Mephisto wasn't so sure. Well, about the labor part anyway. He was definitely sure about her loving pain. Her lips were a little pinched, and her jaw seemed to tighten in response to the sexy, intense scenes around them. He kissed her on the side of the neck. "Don't be too sad, kitten. Our day will come again."

Molly shifted to pull him closer, one hand cradling her distended waist. "No... I'm not sad, Master. I'm a little uncomfortable. I think I might be in labor."

Mephisto blinked. "What? What?!" *Don't panic. You're the Master, you're in charge. Be cool.* "Are you— How long—?" He squeezed her shoulders, probably much too hard. Okay, not exactly cool.

"It's okay, Master," Molly said quickly. "I'm fine. I'm barely feeling the contractions."

"Being in labor is not the time to brag about your pain tolerance!" he yelled.

Molly looked at him like he was nuts. "No, what I mean is they're not that strong yet. I mean, they haven't been. I didn't think it was the real thing. But now...they're starting to get more intense."

"Why didn't you tell me when they first started? How long has this been going on?"

"A few hours now, Master. But it's Friday night...and the club's so busy... Labor can last for twelve hours or more."

He took her chin in his fingers and glared at her. "I'll beat you for this later. I really think I will."

"If you believe I deserve punishment, Master, I'll happily—"

"Oh God," Mephisto snapped, looking to the heavens for sanity. "Save it. Please. Darling..." He softened his voice. "When was your last contraction?"

Her mouth tightened. "I'm having one right now."

"Is it bad? I mean, on the scale of a non-masochistic person?"

"Um...this one is actually pretty bad, Master. Even for me." She opened her mouth and started panting quietly. Mephisto let out a long slow breath. "Holy fuck me. Okay. This is why we have your bag all packed. I'll call Dr. Willetts. Wait here."

The kinksters around them were starting to notice something was going on. Probably from the way Molly was gripping her belly and bending over at the waist.

"This dungeon is not equipped for childbirth, even if it has a medical table and stirrups," Mephisto warned as he ran to the back to grab her bag. By the time he returned, one of the bouncers was waiting with Molly by the door. On the way across the play space, he corralled Lorna by one arm.

"I need you."

"Asking first is nice."

"Lorna, please come with us. She doesn't have a mother to be here. She needs a woman with her, a woman who's been through this before."

Lorna eyed Molly. Mephisto could sense her softening even as she turned to glare at him, lips pursed. "I'm not a mommy, Master Mephisto, as you know. I'm a Mistress."

Mephisto shrugged, drawing her along. "Fortunately, she responds to that too."

* * * * *

Molly was placid even in excruciating pain. Mephisto, though, was about to jump out of his skin. She was suffering so badly, and the contractions were close together now. Molly would screw her eyes shut and whimper through each one, making tiny huffing noises of panic, each one like a stab in his heart. "Why don't you just take something, kitten?"

"It's almost over," she gasped. "It's okay, I can do it."

"This isn't a test. You don't have to prove anything to anyone."

"Yes I do," she said with a surprising amount of heat, before collapsing back in exhaustion. "I have to prove something to myself."

Mistress Lorna glowered from the corner. "Just make her, Mephisto. You're the Master, aren't you?" she added with a hint of derision.

Yes, he was the Master, but in this... He shook his head. "She's the one in labor. Not me."

Lorna sauntered over and leaned down to fix Molly in her stern gaze. "Take the drugs, girl. Have an epidural. Why don't you do it for your Master's peace of mind, instead of being so selfish?"

"It might hurt the baby," Molly gasped.

"Where did you hear that? Poppycock." Mephisto stifled a smile at Lorna's blustering, while Molly's wide eyes took in the domme's threatening glare. There was a reason this woman could subdue even the most intransigent male slaves. "Get an epidural now and you can enjoy the rest of the birth in peace with your Master. Or keep being stubborn. I've been where you are, Molly. It only gets worse. Pretty soon those contractions will be coming right on top of each other, with no time to rest in between."

"Holy hell." Mephisto turned on his heel. "I'm going for a nurse. I'll be right back."

The nurse returned with him a minute later, smiling brightly. "Mr. Tennant tells me you're ready to order an epidural."

"Yes, ma'am," Molly answered meekly. Good girl. A few minutes later he was standing in front of her, bracing her while she whined through another contraction. She sucked in a breath as the anesthesiologist poked at her back.

"Does it hurt?" he asked.

"The epidural, no. The contraction?" She whimpered again. "Yes, it really hurts."

Her soft "it really hurts" was the equivalent of a tortured scream from an average woman.

He leaned his head close to her, trying to give her his comfort, his strength. "I don't know how to handle seeing you endure pain that doesn't turn you on." She panted in his ear, then buried her head in his shoulder. "You gotta have this baby for me. Soon."

"I think it's going to be soon," she sighed. "It's cracking me open."

The nurse and Mephisto helped her lie back. The next contraction came and Mephisto could tell it felt milder to her. By the third one, she was relaxed with a smile on her face. "You should give those epidurals out in the dungeon," she said. "The subs could take a lot more. I can't feel anything."

"You're smiling. Joking. It's a miracle."

"I'm happy, Master. Thanks for making me get the epidural."

Lorna tsked from the corner and rolled her eyes. "Deliver me. Seriously."

"You too, Mistress," Molly chirped. "Thanks for your kind advice."

Lorna spoke out of the side of her mouth to him. "Fascinating," she snarked. "I can hardly believe she's real." She spoke to Molly in a louder voice. "You can show me your thanks on some other occasion perhaps. If your Master permits."

"Really?" Mephisto snorted. "You're going to hit on my slave while she's at eight centimeters?"

"Ten," corrected Molly. "I'm feeling a lot of pressure down there, and the nurse told me that means I might be ready to push."

"Good God. Let's get the nurse then."

"I'll do it," Lorna said. "You stay with your wife and catch the baby if it comes shooting out."

They watched the domme stroll out of the room. Molly's eyes met Mephisto's and he laughed. "Go ahead. Say it."

"I'm just wondering what she was like as a mom."

He stroked her hair. "I'm pretty sure your parenting style won't resemble hers. But I bet she was a good mom, and you will be too. Do you need anything?" he asked. She looked tired, but so beautiful. "I'm so ready for this, Molly. Our baby's coming. No second thoughts?"

Molly shook her head. "I can't wait to see our child. You and me together in a little human being."

Mephisto glanced at his watch. "I think he's going to share your Master's birthday, strange as that is." He paused. "No, not really strange. Clayton always engineered everything. He's probably up on a cloud right now smiling that big 'I control the universe' smile."

"Yes, I can see it. And you said 'he' again, for the baby. You really want a boy, don't you?"

"I told you, kitten, I'll take anything. Maybe a strong little girl like you."

Molly held his gaze. "I'm not strong, Master."

"Aren't you? You're handling this like a champ. Better than I would have." A shriek sounded through the open door from somewhere down the hall. "Better than that woman." He leaned close to whisper in her ear. "You're a good slave, giving birth to my baby."

"I don't want your baby!" Molly whispered back, grinning.

Mephisto burst into laughter. "I'm going to miss that game."

"Why?" asked Molly. "We can still play. And you can be a lot meaner when I'm not really pregnant."

Mephisto felt a tightness of arousal in his middle. "Stop that. You're about to give birth, you wanton. Don't turn me on."

They both fell silent as Lorna returned with the OB nurse. "Would you like to watch in the mirror?" the nurse asked.

Molly shook her head, horrified.

180

Another nurse entered with a baby warmer and bunch of serious looking gear. After she got that situated, she helped Molly prop herself up. The bottom of the hospital bed came off. It was all happening awfully fast. Now, finally, Lorna was on her feet at Molly's side, so his wife had a dreadlocked satyr on one side of her bed and a leather-corseted dominatrix on the other as she began to push.

At this too, she was a natural. Mephisto cursed and Lorna wheedled and browbeat the stubborn baby in turn, but Molly was utterly sedate through the whole process. Now and again, Mephisto's gaze caught on the silver collar around her neck. She'd refused to take it off, even at the urging of the first shift nurse. If he got his way, she would never take it off.

Push, relax. Wait. Push, relax. Wait. As the ordeal stretched on for twenty, thirty, forty minutes, Lorna became the mom she pretended not to be. She stroked Molly's face, urged her on with gentle encouragements. Finally Dr. Willetts breezed in wearing delivery scrubs, pulling on gloves. He gave Molly the praise that Mephisto was too overwrought to summon up.

"You make this look easy, Mrs. Tennant." Molly was bearing down, concentrating. Her strain and exhaustion showed on her face, but she grasped their hands and kept smiling. *Smiling.* And just like that, in her silent, persevering way, without any rants or screams or moans, she brought their child into the world. Molly cried, Lorna bawled, and even Mephisto felt his eyes tearing up.

The baby was...scary looking. A little red, a little blue, a little messy. A lot messy. There was a cry and a wail that sounded completely alien to Mephisto, and yet was the most awe-inspiring sound in the world.

"It's a boy," said Dr. Willetts. "Do you have a name picked out yet?"

Mephisto and Molly exchanged looks. "We didn't know what we were having," Mephisto explained. "So, no. Not yet."

"He looks just like you," Molly sighed as the nurses laid the baby across her stomach. Wonder of wonders, he did, as much as a shriveled-up, wailing baby boy could look like a grown man. Molly gazed at Mephisto and smiled, looking very proud of herself. "I knew you wanted a boy."

* * * * *

Her Master was too nervous to hold him for a while, which she understood completely. Molly was nervous too. Luckily Lorna was there to reassure her, and the two of them alternately cooed over and snuggled the tiny bundle. The baby looked much better now that he was cleaned up. And yes, he was his father's son. His bold features were little miniatures of Mephisto's. As Lorna jokingly said, her Master's genes had dommed Molly's into submission.

When Lorna finally ordered Mephisto over to hold his son in his arms, he reached for him gingerly. The baby was so tiny and fragile. So light, like a feather. It frightened her, the vulnerability of their delicate child.

But then, Molly always thought herself weak and vulnerable too—but now she felt so, so strong. She had to be strong now. Already, after just a couple hours, she'd fallen in love with her son. She'd do anything for him, anything on earth, and she had to be strong to take care of him. Not that she was worried. Everything felt right. She was tired but happy, and her beloved Master was holding their baby, rocking him gently in the rocker beside the hospital bed.

"He's so beautiful, kitten," he said. "You did a really great job."

Molly flushed at his worshipful tone. "I couldn't have done it without you."

Mistress Lorna laughed. "Literally. But I think you did most of the hard work, little slavegirl." Molly's eyes widened as the brassy Mistress thunked her Master square on the head. "Now you'll need to let her rest. Get up for the night time feedings. The Master/slave thing doesn't apply when there's a newborn in the house. For now, you serve her."

Molly thought that sounded crazy, but then she realized it would have to be that way for a while. She couldn't do both...take care of a newborn and be a perfect slave. But it was Master Mephisto who'd convinced her, finally, that she didn't have to be a perfect slave all the time. That she could be Molly too, sometimes, and everything in the world would still be okay. It was a long sought, deeply relieving realization. She would adore him forever for that alone.

Oh, and for how tenderly he held their baby...

"Earth to Molly." Lorna waved a perfectly manicured hand in front of Molly's face. "Did you hear what I said?"

Molly smiled. "Yes. I have to make my Master do everything for the next few days."

"The next few *weeks*," Lorna corrected her. "I'm serious, girl. I know enough about you to know you push things too far sometimes. Now you're making choices for two. Motherhood comes first, always. Well, until your baby's out of the newborn stage. Then you two can work on striking a balance."

Her Master regarded the dominatrix with a sardonic smile. "Yes, Mistress. I live to obey."

"You live to irritate me, Mephisto." She looked at her watch. "I suppose I should swing by my shop to be sure everyone's behaving, and to start spreading the news, if you don't mind?"

"That would be great, Lorna, thank you. And thanks for coming to help out tonight."

"Yes, thank you, Mistress," Molly echoed. "You helped me so much."

After giving one last snuggle to the baby and congratulatory hugs to both of them, Mistress Lorna was gone. Molly's Master placed their slumbering baby into his isolette and turned down the lights. "You should sleep while he sleeps. That's what the nurse said."

"But I don't want you to go."

"I'm not going." He crawled onto the narrow hospital bed and spooned behind her. She relaxed back into his solid warmth, feeling the last of the lingering tension in her arms and neck fade away. She fingered her cool metal collar as he nuzzled her, dropping a kiss behind her ear.

"Sleep, Molly." He reached out to touch the metal-rail sides of the bed. "Think of this as your cage."

She took his hand. "You're my cage, Master. I love you."

"I adore you, little kitten. Now obey me. Sleep."

She tried, but she couldn't quite settle down. After about ten minutes, she whispered in the darkness, "Master, are you still awake?"

"Yes."

"He doesn't have a name yet. I can't sleep without knowing what to call him. Shouldn't we decide?"

"Hmm." Mephisto drew in a deep breath and let it out slowly. "Marvin?"

She giggled. "That's awful. Anyway, we agreed, no 'M' names. Molly and Mephisto is already a tongue-twister."

"Yes," he said, licking her earlobe. "But you go by kitten most of the time. How about Walter?"

Molly wrinkled her nose. "Um."

"Jethro? Wolfgang? Hoboken?" Her Master put a hand over her mouth as she burst into laughter. "Shhh."

"You're kidding, I hope," she whispered.

"Cthulhu?"

She choked back another laugh behind his fingers, then peeled his hand away. "That kind of works. It goes with the whole Mephisto thing."

"If we're thinking along those lines, we could go with Beelzebub, or Archfiend—Archie for short. Diablo. Hell, we could be really subversive and name him Satan."

"Not my baby. He's too sweet for that."

"You're right. We'll go with Hoboken."

They laughed another moment or two, then her Master sobered. "I would suggest Clayton, but I'm not sure I could stand our son having the same name as your former Master. Kind of squicks me."

Molly shuddered. "Yeah, me too." She drew her fingers up his strong, hair-roughened forearm, then down again to lace with his fingers. "You know, I'm kind of partial to Jonathan. I always have been, I don't know why."

Her Master considered a moment. "Jonathan. I like it. My real name also starts with a J."

"I know." Molly felt intensely sleepy all of a sudden, now that the big decision was made. Their sweet baby Jonathan. She liked the formality of the name, and the way it could become Jon, or Jonny, depending on the kind of little boy he grew into. That was still a mystery. There was so much to come. Would his eyes stay deep blue like Molly's, or turn dark like her Master's? Would he be short or tall, reserved or active, creative or sensible? "Do you think he'll be a lot like you?" Molly asked just before she drifted off.

"I don't know, baby." He pressed another kiss against her shoulder. "I only know I want him to be as happy as me," he added in a quiet afterthought.

As happy as both of them. Safe in her Master's arms, Molly fell into a deep and dreamless sleep.

EPILOGUE

Her Master walked with her along the cool, tree-lined lane. It was late August; Jonathan was already three and half months old. Master pushed him in the stroller while Molly carried her violin case.

"It's been a while since we were here." Her Master looked around at the solid, gray tombstones. "But it still looks the same. Not much changes in a cemetery."

"Kind of comforting, isn't it?" Molly murmured.

Jonathan peered around in his stroller, clutching his favorite blankey in one hand. He was an easy baby, laid back and cuddly. He looked more like his father every day. His eyes changed to a medium brown and his headful of dark hair looked very dashing. People always called him a beautiful baby, but Molly thought beautiful didn't even cut it.

Mephisto parked the stroller a short distance away and reached into the basket underneath for the flowers and gardening tools they'd brought. They worked wordlessly side by side, cutting back the bulbs that had bloomed in the spring when they'd been too busy and too pregnant to keep up with these visits. Afterward the baby had kept them running around the clock, and when things settled down, there was the necessary re-connection with each other. As a result, Clayton had been neglected until now.

They'd brought vibrant colored flowers. Petunias in fuchsia, pink, purple. Her Master held them up so Jonathan could bat at them. The baby's eyes drank in the colors. Then Mephisto knelt and dug little holes for Molly to fill. She looked down at him, her beautiful partner, with his strong back and shoulders, his riot of dreadlocks. They'd brushed across her cheek that morning, those dreadlocks. Across her back, between her legs. She flushed and shivered a little, remembering. Such pleasure...and a little pain too. They were getting back into it. It was her Master who wanted to take things slowly, who seemed to find new vulnerability in her now that she was the mother of his child.

But they would find their way. She had a few slave tricks up her sleeve, and by now, she was getting pretty skilled at what made her Master tick, what wound him up and made him do the most evil, delicious things to her.

She still missed her old Master. Now and again things would remind her of him and she'd feel the pang of his loss. Not things like the meetings she still attended to carry on his business, but things like a look from her present Master, or a particularly hard spanking that moved her to tears. A tender kiss, a stroke of fingers down her cheek, and she'd remember another time, another place with the same feeling, the same fullness in her heart.

She'd have to tell Clayton all this some time when Mephisto wasn't there. Not that he would object. They were just private feelings, memories for Clayton alone.

They patted down the last of the soil around the petunias. They wouldn't last the winter, but they'd be able to visit more frequently from now on. They could put in more flowers in the spring. Jonathan might be walking by then, or at least getting close.

"Do you want me to leave him here so you can introduce him to Clayton?"

Molly looked down at her baby, then back at him. "That would be kind of silly, wouldn't it?"

He shrugged. "Jonathan likes to hear you play. Why don't you keep him with you?"

"Yes, Master." Molly was grateful he'd spared her the embarrassment of having to ask. Because, silly or not, she wanted to introduce her baby to Clayton, even if Clayton wasn't really there. Or maybe he was there somehow. Molly always felt closest to him here, his picturesque gravesite like some earth-to-afterlife portal between them.

"I'll leave you three alone," her Master said, pressing a kiss on her temple. "Take your time."

Molly played first, soft, soothing violin music. She played for Jonathan a lot. The sweet resonant notes of the violin seemed to have the power to soothe him when nothing else could. Mephisto tried to replicate the effect with recorded music a couple times while Molly was away, but apparently digital violin music didn't relax him quite the same. Molly wondered if it had something to do with the movement of the bow across the strings or her particular style of playing. Anyway, she was glad her old Master had made her learn, and her new Master had encouraged her to keep trying, and that she hadn't been successful in smashing her violin those many months ago.

By the time she finished her short concert, the baby was fast asleep in his stroller and Mephisto was looking pretty drowsy himself over in the shady glade where he waited. He'd laid down on the lengthy bench and slung a hand over his eyes. It was a perfect day for relaxing outdoors and enjoying fresh air. Molly sat in the spongy green grass over her old Master's grave and soon found herself stretched out in the sun too. She rolled onto her side, brushing the slender soft green blades.

"Hello, Master," she whispered. "It's Molly. I'm sure you know that already, from the violin playing. It's a beautiful day today. Sorry I haven't been to see you more often. I found out I was pregnant." She closed her eyes and ripped up a few blades of grass, scattering them around. "I was angry to find out you misled me about the sterilization. But I'm glad now you did it the way you did, because I did end up wanting a baby. Thanks for leaving me that choice." She looked over at her slumbering son. "I have a beautiful boy named Jonathan. He loves music and he looks just like your old friend Mephisto."

At that moment, Jonathan made one of his sweet funny baby faces in his sleep. What was he dreaming about? What had Molly dreamed about at that age? Probably simple, wonderful things. Things she wanted, that she eventually got. Love and belonging. She was a lucky girl, because she'd gotten them twice, along with much, much more.

"I'm doing great otherwise. I'm still volunteering, but fewer days a week now. Mrs. Jernigan helps watch the baby. You wouldn't believe how sweet she is with him. She was always such a bitch to me." Molly slapped a hand over her mouth. "Sorry, Master. But she was. Oh, and guess what? My friend Eliot graduates next year in the spring. He's in law school on your dime, some fancy university in New York. You remember, we talked about it earlier? I still meet with him now and again. He decided to specialize in family law. We used to talk a lot about my adventures at the Family Center, and he says that's why he decided to go into that. You know, to help."

She bit her lip, smoothing down the grass she'd been pulling at. "He reminds me a lot of you, only he's about 99% less kinky. Maybe 100%. But he's still a great guy. You would have liked him if you met him. I wish you could have met him." Her throat tightened as she sat up to look at his name, and those horrible dates. That heart underneath that represented such love but still made her so sad. "I wish I could have shared all this with you while you were alive. I wish you could have been here with me for longer. You know, I still have your collar. I hold it sometimes and I—I miss you so much. I know you loved me, truly loved me, and I'll always love you."

It was all she could say. She started bawling—her post-pregnancy hormones still flared up her emotions sometimes. She crawled closer, careful not to crush the delicate flowers they'd just planted. She put her forehead right against his cold granite stone, her fingers tracing over the black etched letters of his name. She didn't realize how hard she was crying until she felt a warm wall behind her, and her Master pulling her into his arms.

"Oh, Molly," he said softly. "I miss him too."

Molly wiped at her tears, embarrassed. God, it had been over a year now. Why did his loss still hurt so bad? She gazed up at her Master, not wanting him to think she was unhappy when she was so content with him, so fulfilled. "It's not that I don't love you terribly, I just—"

"Shh. It's okay. I know you love me, and I know you love him too. I think you can love many people in a lifetime. I think the more people you love, the happier you are, you know?"

Molly nodded, sniffling. She tried to collect herself. It was okay. Everything was okay. "You won't leave me?" she blurted out. "Master, you won't die for a long, long time, will you?"

"Not for ages, kitten. I'll live to be at least a hundred. I can be stubborn that way."

Jonathan stirred, perhaps roused by the rumble of his papa's voice. They both looked over at him as his eyes popped open. As soon as he saw them, he gave a crooked smile. Mephisto chuckled, then looked back at her. "We shouldn't worry about things like that right now. We'll take it one day at a time." He picked up her violin case. "Play a little more for me, and then we'd better get back before Jonathan gets too hungry."

Molly took out her violin and played for love and loss, for change and growth, for the heat of desire, and all the surprises of life. She realized as she played that she didn't play nearly often enough for her new Master who'd brought so much richness to her life. She would play for him more, she vowed.

But for now she played for both of them—the first Master who made her, and the second Master who saved her. Somehow they both fit in her heart, with room for a beautiful baby too. *I think the more people you love, the happier you are, you know?*

Yes, Master, I know... Molly drew her bow across the strings, drawing out the last lingering note, staring into her Master's dark, adoring eyes.

A FINAL NOTE

I hope you enjoyed the conclusion to Molly and Mephisto's saga. If you haven't read the "prequels" to this book, *Club Mephisto* and *Molly's Lips: Club Mephisto Retold*, perhaps you will. While they are not as romantic as this story, they shed a lot of light on Molly and Mephisto's past and Molly's relationship with Clayton Copeland, her first Master.

I have a deep admiration for those who are called to practice intense M/s and power exchange. Molly and Mephisto are an homage to those friends, but also, hopefully, a canvas on which to display the human struggles of that kind of dynamic. I have great respect also for those who love intensely, and this book is an homage to them as well.

To learn more about *Club Mephisto*, *Molly's Lips*, and my other novels, please visit my website at www.annabeljoseph.com. You can also follow me on Twitter (@annabeljoseph) or "like" my Facebook page at www.facebook.com/annabeljosephnovels.

ABOUT THE AUTHOR

Annabel Joseph is a multi-published BDSM romance author. She writes mainly contemporary romance, although she has been known to dabble in the medieval and Regency eras. She is known for writing emotionally intense BDSM storylines, and strives to create characters that seem real—even flawed—so readers are better able to relate to them.

Annabel Joseph loves to hear from her readers at
annabeljosephnovels@gmail.com.

An excerpt from *Command Performance*, the fourth and final book in the Comfort series, coming from Annabel Joseph in the fall of 2012

Mason climbed into the studio car, a luxury he took for granted after ten years headlining movies. He wished he could tell the driver to head to LoveSlave, the elite underground dungeon his friends frequented. He could pick up some horny, starstruck subbie and fuck her senseless through a night of hedonistic play...but that was impossible. The tabloids paid too much for kiss-and-tell stories these days, and after a night with him, the woman would have way too much to tell. He didn't dare hire a professional call girl for the same reason.

If it wasn't for one very special friend, he would have lost his mind by now. After the chauffeur shuttled him to his home in Malibu, Mason hopped into his own car and dialed her number. After a few rings, a familiar voice answered. "Hello?"

"Satya, my love."

"Mason Cooke, do you have any idea how late it is?" Her clipped tones sounded like music in his ear.

"I know it's late. I had a hard day."

"Oh, did you?" Her voice dripped derision. He and Satya were long time friends, childhood friends, and their dynamic was...unique. Two years ago he couldn't have imagined any romance between them. Well, there *was* no romance between them, but in the dark days after Jessamine left him, and after Satya had been dumped by a long time love, they'd started hooking up in secret. Extreme secret. Even Kai, Mason's best friend and Satya's protective older brother, still wasn't aware it was going on.

It had been by mutual agreement, the subterfuge. Mason and Satya were friends, and both of them knew they could never be anything else. Mason had confessed his kinky proclivities to her, which she did not share, and she was too focused on her human rights work to get caught up in the tabloid storm that was his life. But as long as he was vanilla with her—and discreet—he was welcome in her bed when things got rough.

"So what was so hard about your day?" Satya asked. "Was your martini lunch shaken rather than stirred? They run out of jelly doughnuts on the catering cart?"

"Why are you so mean to me?"

"Oh, I got it. The makeup grunt poked you in the eye while applying your mascara."

"I had to pretend to rape this girl today. Over and over."

Satya tsked. "What girl? Is this more of your perverted shit?"

"It was for the movie I'm working on. *Revelation*."

"Oh, yeah. Who was the lucky victim of this exploitation?"

"Mireille Donovan."

Satya made a squicked sound. "You had to rape her? She's what, fifteen years old?"

"She's actually in her twenties now. But it was still horrible."

"When is Hollywood going to get tired of rape-as-entertainment? And I suppose you're too traumatized to spend the night alone?"

"Please, Sats." Mason wasn't above begging. He'd done it before.

"You know," she sighed, "when I get a boyfriend, all this ends. It has to."

"I know."

"You won't be able to call me at eleven at night with your sob stories. *Satya, I'm so horny!*"

Her impression was dead on, but he didn't feel like laughing. "Please let me come over." Mason lowered his voice to a seductive whisper. "You know I'll make it worth your while."

"Okay," she finally said. "But no sleeping over. I don't want to wake up next to your ugly mug. I have to go to work in the morning."

"Fine, no sleeping over. I'll be there in five minutes." Mason hung up and relaxed, watching for the turnoff to her little bungalow in the hills. He did a quick sweep for hiding paparazzi before he parked and hurried to her door. She'd already unlocked it for him; he took the stairs to her bedroom two at a time.

"Stop." She held up a hand as he came toward her bed. "You leave all the rape and whatnot at the doorstep. Understand?"

"I love when you scold me," Mason murmured, stripping off his clothes. "When you make me feel like a bad little boy."

He launched himself at her, and she fought him, shrieking. "You are a bad little boy!"

"Not a boy anymore," he grunted. "Want me to show you?"

"Oh, Mason," she sighed as he slid his pelvis across her mound. "Not little either..."

Satya was fun to have sex with. They played in bed together more than made love. Mason knew Satya was right, that they had no future together as a couple, but he treasured what she allowed him to share. He took his time winding her up, stroking her, teasing her to a frenzy of horniness before he rolled on a condom and slid between her legs.

"Do you want me?" His hands played over her hips, her waist. Her lovely dark-tipped breasts. "Do you want me deep inside you?"

She didn't answer, only grabbed his ass and drew him into her. They moved together, enjoying one another with leisurely caresses and whispers. Mason urged her on until she came, and then he made her come again. His staying power was legendary, which he believed made him an especially good lover. It gave him more time to focus on his partner. He rarely heard women complain.

Well, Satya complained. As soon as they finished, she pushed him off, as usual, so she could lie solitary and replete in the afterglow. When he tried to kiss her, she swatted him and told him to go away.

So Mason went away. It was an arrangement that worked for them. On the way out to the car he turned his phone back on and found seven messages from his publicist. Make that eight.

Crisis. You need to call me ASAP. Re: your depraved sex life.

With a sinking heart, Mason dialed Shane Greenberg's number. "Hi, Shane. Did you mean that message as a proposition?"

"This isn't funny, my friend. My phone's lighting up, messages from all the tabs and the online gossip sites too. Someone sold a story, not just about you, but about all your kinky Hollywood buddies. Tales about partner swapping, dungeons, bondage, orgies, all kinds of craziness. There are photos too."

"Orgy photos?" Mason's heart hammered.

"What the— Really, Mace? There are orgy photos out there somewhere?"

"Uh, no. Well, probably not."

A long sigh sounded over the line. "The ones I saw were just party-type photos. Provocative, but not damning. Several producers and movie execs were named too, but you and Jeremy Gray are the celebrities, so you're the ones everyone will talk about. And Jeremy is married, a family man. With a kid."

"So he'll look worse than me?"

"No, better, because it will look like he's settled down from all that nonsense. You, on the other hand, just got divorced."

"From Jessamine Jackson! She's the sexual deviant, not me." A bit of a lie. "I mean, she was ten times more promiscuous than I was. I hope she's being dragged down in all this too."

"This person claims Jess divorced you because you were into sado-masochism and she wasn't. The source paints Jess as the victim to your sick sex demands."

Jesus Christ. That was so untrue. Yes, he'd been into BDSM and Jess hadn't been, but they'd broken up over a whole hell of a lot more than that.

"Is all this legit?" Shane's strident voice interrupted the hurtful memories. "Talk to me, Mason. Orgies, kinky sex, partner swapping parties with twenty or more people?"

"Twenty is kind of an exaggeration."

"Is it true?" Shane barked.

"It's...possibly true."

"Come on!"

"Okay, yes, that stuff goes on. But we've been discreet. I don't know who would be out there talking about this. Not Jessamine?"

"If it was Jessamine, they would have revealed her as the source to make it an even bigger story. But it's a killer as it is. You're the all-American movie star. The hunky, relatable guy. Now everyone's going to be picturing you in a black leather mask with a whip, presiding over orgies."

"Jessamine always ran the orgies."

His publicist made a sound like his brain was exploding. "Mason, goddamn it."

"Okay! Okay. So what do you suggest I do?"

"Don't open your door. Don't talk to any reporters. Lay low for a while and hope it disappears quickly, that people are too embarrassed to talk about it. Don't even leave your house."

"I'm working on a movie!"

"Oh yeah." Shane sighed again, heavy and long. "A movie about a sick, sexually deranged individual, if I remember correctly."

"I'm afraid so."

"Jesus Christ. You don't pay me enough for this shit."

"I know." Mason turned onto his street, cursed for a full fifteen seconds, and turned a corner to go the other way. The front of his house was crawling with media trucks and paparazzi. The gate was blocked by photographers in a line, waiting for the money shot. He wouldn't be safe at a hotel. As soon as he checked in, someone would call whatever pap was in their pocket. He couldn't go to Jeremy's house, or Kai's, or any of his friends who had probably been named in the scandal, because they would be blanketed with paparazzi too. Anything sex related became a media feeding frenzy. This was bad, really bad.

He'd have to sleep in his trailer on the movie set, if he could even get on the lot at this hour.

He was fucked.

The Comfort series is:

Comfort Object (Jeremy and Nell's story, 2009)

Caressa's Knees (Kyle and Caressa's story, 2011)

Odalisque (Kai and Constance's story, 2011)

and *Command Performance*, Mason and Miri's story, coming in the fall of 2012 to an e-tailer near you!

Made in the USA
San Bernardino, CA
22 March 2016